Outback

The Visitor

ANNIE SEATON

The Augathella Girls: Book 6

This book is a work of fiction. Names, characters, places, magazine and incidents are the product of the author's imagination or are used fictitiously. Any resemblance to actual events, locales, or persons, living or dead, is coincidental.

Copyright © 2022 Annie Seaton

All rights reserved.

ISBN 978-0-6454843-1-1

THE AUGATHELLA GIRLS

Book 1: <u>Outback Roads – The Nanny</u>

Book 2: <u>Outback Sky – The Pilot</u>

Book 3: <u>Outback Escape – The Sister</u>

Book 4: <u>Outback Winds – The Jillaroo</u>

Book 5: <u>Outback Dawn – The Visitor</u>

Book 6: <u>Outback Moonlight – The Rogue</u>

Book 7: <u>Outback Dust – The Drifter</u>

Book 8: <u>Outback Hope – The Farmer</u>

Augathella Characters - Book 6

Jacinta Mason	Teacher
Ryan Francesco	Male revue staff
Harry Higgins	Doctor
Laura Adnum	Midwife
Brad and Callie Cartwright	*Kilcoy Station*
Kent Mason / Sophie Cartwright	*Lara Waters*
Jon Ingram/Fallon Malone & Ryan	Station manager & family
Bec Hunter	Nurse
Ben Riley and Amelia Foley	Shire engineer & station hand
Bram, Hilly, Chappo, and Slim	Male revue staff
Clive	Tour manager

Chapter 1

Jacinta

Jacinta Mason walked slowly along the path to the maxi taxi waiting outside her front gate. She could hear the laughter coming from inside the vehicle and tried to fight the dread rising in her stomach.

The last thing she wanted was to go on a girls' night out. She loved all the girls and she knew she couldn't let Sophie down on her hen's night, especially since she was going to be her bridesmaid in two weeks.

Going to the pub to an all-male revue did not appeal at all. Jacinta was horrified when Sophie told her what the hen's night entailed.

She'd shaken her head. 'Oh my God, Sophie, I'm not going to one of them. They're awful.'

'How do you know that, Jace?' Sophie said,

'Have you ever been to one?'

'No, I haven't, but I've seen them on television.'

Sophie chuckled. 'So, you're a closet male revue watcher.'

'No! I'm not. I just saw one on an ad one day.'

'Well, this one, apparently, is a very professional outfit. It's like that one that garden guy from TV used to be in years and years ago. Remember him?'

'No, and I don't want to go.'

'You're my bridesmaid, Jacinta Mason, and it's up to you to look after the bride at her hen's night. Kent would never forgive you if I drank too much and got sick, or fell over and had a broken leg for the wedding. It's up to you and Callie and Kimberly to make sure that I behave.'

Jacinta had rolled her eyes. 'Well, if you put it like that, I guess I'll have to come.'

Now the taxi was waiting outside her house and she had no choice. She'd offered to meet them at the hotel, but Sophie had shaken her head and looked at her sceptically. 'Nope, we're all arriving together.'

Jacinta thought long and hard about what was suitable attire for a hen's night, but in the end, she realised it didn't matter. This was Sophie's night; she put aside her doubts and fears and concentrated on having a good night.

Winter was fading and the weather had started to warm up already, so she pulled out the usual little black dress that she kept for school functions.

In honour of it being a fun night, Jacinta had bought some coloured beads and fancy earrings at the pharmacy after school yesterday.

She slipped on a pair of flat black shoes because if things got too raunchy and she didn't want to stay, she would take herself off and walk home and the other girls could look after Sophie and make sure she behaved herself. Not that she had any fear of Sophie doing anything wrong because she wasn't much of a drinker anyway.

The girls squealed as she climbed into the back of the taxi and Jacinta stared at the esky on the floor between them.

Sophie pulled out a plastic champagne glass, filled it to the brim and handed it over. 'Hi, Jacinta, welcome to my hen's night.'

'It's going be a big one isn't it, girls? We've got to make it a double whammy seeing Callie and Braden snuck off and got married, and *she* didn't have one.'

'Oh no,' Callie said. 'I'm the responsible married lady here. I'm the matron of honour!'

Jacinta brightened. 'So, you don't need me?' she asked hopefully.

'Even if you hate every minute of the show, it's the company that matters. We're celebrating my marriage to your brother. That's what we're here for tonight.'

'I thought we were celebrating that at the wedding,' Jacinta said.

'Don't be such a wet blanket, Jace. We're going to have a great night.'

An hour later, Jacinta had settled in. A second glass of champagne had relaxed her and watching the roadies set up the show had reassured her. It seemed to be a high-quality set and the music was not too loud.

Yet.

The lights dimmed and Sophie put her hand out. 'Ssh, girls, it's about to start. Now you all have to behave. Okay?'

Jacinta grinned at her. 'You're the one who's going to behave, Sophie Cartwright. I don't want to have to go back and tell my brother you were up dancing with semi-naked men.'

'Oh, it's not like that,' Sophie said. 'It's a very classy show. I saw a video of it. I should've shown you.'

'No thanks.' Jacinta pulled a face.

'Prude.' Sophie's smile was cheeky, and Jacinta pulled a face at her sister-in-law.

The lights went out, and as they came back on, a puff of smoke drifted out from either side of the stage. A man yelled out a welcome and then the loud call was followed by a loud guitar riff. All the women in the pub whooped, and hands drummed on the tables. The noise in the pub was louder than Jacinta had ever heard it.

'Bring it on,' called out Jules from IGA.

Jacinta rolled her eyes; she couldn't believe the women who were here tonight. It looked like every female over eighteen in town—as well as all the surrounding stations from Mitchell to Tambo—had come along. Many of the mothers from school were here, and Jacinta was sure she'd spotted Jennifer Shaw, the school counsellor, on the way in. Jennifer had turned away and tried to look inconspicuous, but Jacinta had picked her easily. She shook her head: Jennifer lived down in Charleville! Surely she hadn't come all this way for a strip show?

Anyway, the pub was packed and there were three staff behind the bar instead of the usual one. A good money spinner for the pub and the town, she guessed as she tried to relax, hoping that it would make the night go quicker.

They hadn't eaten dinner but Callie had ordered three bowls of hot chips from the bar to soak up the alcohol that was being consumed at a fairly steady rate.

'Good,' Jacinta said. 'Now, Soph, if I'm here to make sure you behave, I'm going to make sure you do.'

'Yes, Mum.'

The volume of the music increased and the smoke got thicker. Suddenly the song segued into "YMCA", one of Jacinta's favourite dancing songs when she used to dance in her teens.

Six men—all with their clothes on, thank goodness—the cowboy in a red and black checked shirt, the Indian, the policeman, the bikie, the construction worker, and one she couldn't remember what he was supposed to be from her teenage memories, danced out from each side of the stage and formed a single line.

Jacinta was transfixed by the acrobatics and their dancing and had to agree with Sophie, this *was* a quality show.

Sophie met her eyes across the table and mouthed at her, 'Told you.'

Jacinta settled back into her chair and picked up

her drink and watched the dancing.

The guys were in great shape and were excellent dancers.

Her gaze narrowed and her heart began to beat heavily in her chest as her gaze moved on to the second dancer in the middle. The cowboy.

No.

She closed her eyes; it was just a blast from the past. The music was firing up her memories. Opening her eyes again, she stared at the face of the middle dancer.

Dread coiled over her in a heavy black wave and she blinked to clear her vision. As she stared, she picked up her drink and sculled it.

'Way to go, Jacinta!' Sophie called across the table.

Jacinta closed her eyes and put her hand on her chest as the alcohol fizzed through her veins.

It wasn't him.

It couldn't be.

There was no way that Ryder Francesco would have found his way to Augathella. And certainly not as a dancer in an all-male revue.

She shrank back as the music stopped and the dancers approached their table.

Absolutely no way. He didn't even know she lived here.

Jacinta leaned over to Sophie and spoke above the music. 'I'm going outside to get some air.' She jumped up and fled for the door.

Chapter 2

Jacinta

Jacinta pushed the door open, hardly able to see anything around her. As she stepped out into the fresh air, her breathing eased a little and she took a deep breath.

I'm overreacting, she told herself. *There's no way that could be Ryder.*

There was no way he'd be here in Augathella. It was the last place he'd come; he knew she'd lived here once. And after what he'd done to her, he'd avoid the town like the plague.

Jacinta walked over to the back of the pub where two barbecue tables sat on the lawn along the paddock side. She jumped as a voice came from behind her as she stared out over the dark paddocks.

'Jacinta? Are you okay?' Bec Hunter's dark hair shone in the light at the end of the building.

'Oh hi, Bec. Yes . . . yes, um, I just needed

some air.'

'Are you sure? You looked absolutely stricken as you ran out. I was worried you weren't feeling well.'

'No, no. I'm fine. Sort of fine, anyway. It was hot and noisy in there and I just . . . um . . . I just thought . . . I thought I saw someone on the stage I knew a long time ago and it threw me. I needed some time out to calm down and tell myself how stupid I was being.'

'It more than threw you. You looked like you were about to have a heart attack,' Bec said.

'Did the other girls notice?' Jacinta asked, worried she'd drawn attention to herself. That was not something she liked to do. She was quite happy in her kindergarten room with a class full of little ones, and then a night at home alone, preparing the lessons for the next day. Since she'd moved back home from Brisbane, her life had been quiet and she'd learned to be satisfied with her own company. Her confidence had taken a big hit in the city, and Jacinta wasn't prepared to put herself in that position again. If she didn't mix, there was no risk of getting hurt.

'No, they're all having a ball. They were watching the guys. Between you and me, it's absolutely not my scene. I'd rather be tucked up at home with a good book.'

'You and me both, Bec. What have we turned into? Staid old ladies already?' Jacinta managed a smile.

'You'd be surprised.' Bec grinned. 'There's quite a few of the staid older ladies from town in there. They must have arrived after us. Geraldine from the post office was being pulled up on the stage just as I came out.'

'Geraldine?' Jacinta widened her eyes. 'Geraldine Munsey? Oh, how embarrassing.'

'Yes! And that's not all. Jennifer Shaw from your school was putting her hand up to be chosen. She was screaming out, "Pick me, pick me".'

'Oh my gosh.' Jacinta shook her head unable to believe that a professional woman would behave like that in public. 'Really? She must have had a few wines.'

'Really. But's actually it's not a bad show. I was expecting the worst. I went to one when I was at uni that left little to the imagination, but this one is fairly classy.' Bec looked at her curiously. 'Who did you think you saw?'

Jacinta bit her lip and hesitated. No one in Augathella knew about Ryder and what happened in Brisbane two years ago. She'd just wanted to come home and lick her wounds when he'd left her. Eventually, she shook her head slightly. 'No one. It doesn't matter.'

'If someone makes you look like a ghost, I think it does,' Bec said. 'If it doesn't matter, why are you so upset?'

Jacinta trusted Bec; they'd been friends since primary school and had both come back to town after university. Bec because she wanted to, Jacinta because she needed to. She knew if she told Bec about her naivety and her subsequent humiliation, it wouldn't go any further. She hesitated and then decided it wouldn't hurt. After all, Bec had been concerned and kind enough to come out and check she was okay.

'Remember when I came back home after uni and everyone was surprised because they thought I was going to stay in the city? Well, I did intend to stay in Brisbane, but—'

But?' Bec prompted.

'Something happened to me and I felt like such a fool, I needed to get away. I lost all my judgement, and trust in people. So, home was the logical destination. I guess I wanted the comfort of familiar territory. Where I felt safe.'

'What was the something that happened?' Bec asked gently. 'You weren't assaulted, were you, Jace?'

'No, nothing like that.'

The evening had descended and the darkness enveloping them made it a little easier for Jacinta to answer honestly. She took a deep breath and ignored the pain that pierced her heart. The pain that she'd managed to keep at bay for almost three years. That's how long it had taken her to get over

Ryder. Almost three long years of waiting for him to find her, and tell her it had all been a mistake. Last year after the Christmas holidays, she'd given herself a stern talking to, and stopped thinking about him. And now look what had happened.

'I was going out with this guy and we broke up. It was awful. I'd kidded myself that I loved him, and he loved me, and I had already begun to paint a picture of our life together in my head. You know what a dreamer I was.'

'You were always a romantic. That's why I've been surprised to see how you barely socialise these days. When we were at high school, you were the life and soul of the party. Lots of parties from memory. So why did you break up?'

'Well, it wasn't technically a breakup. I guess you can't call it that when a guy just walks out on you, can you? Break-up sounds mutual. And civilised. And it sounds better than saying someone just walked out because you're not what he thought you were.' Jacinta gave a self-deprecating laugh. 'And when it happens after the first night you ever sleep together, it's not real crash hot for the ego.'

'The rotten sod,' Bec said. 'It obviously hit you hard if you haven't got over it after . . . how long?'

'Two and a half years. You'd think I would have by now.'

'How long were you together?'

'I knew him for six months. It was a slow-growing relationship; we started off as friends and then it took off from there. Ryder had two jobs and I was working on the other side of the city after I finished my last exams and waiting for my results. We saw each other a couple of times a week to start with. I was so naïve, Bec. I was convinced it was the real thing. I fell hard and I thought I'd found my soulmate. The nights we didn't see each other, he'd call and we'd talk for hours. He was . . . or I thought he was . . . such a lovely guy. I should have known when he avoided staying the night that there was someone else. I still haven't figured out why he hung around with me.' She laughed again and it was bitter. 'It sure wasn't for the sex because there wasn't any.'

'What happened?'

'The last night I saw him, we slept together; when I woke up, he was gone. I never saw or heard from him again. He certainly did a number on me. I'd had very little experience with guys before Ryder.' She pulled a face. 'There was only one guy before him in year twelve, and after that I was focused on my study. I guess it showed. I haven't been out with a guy since then. Totally lost my confidence.'

'Oh, sweetie. How awful and what a shit way to treat you. Now that I know why you're a stay-at-home gal, we'll have to get you out and about.'

'I'm out and about tonight, Bec. Reluctantly and now look what's happened. I see someone who looks like a jerk from my past and I have a panic attack. I should be well and truly over it. In fact, I very rarely give Ryder a thought these days, but seeing his double in a male revue was a shock.'

Okay, maybe that wasn't quite the truth, but it made her sound less of a tragic.

'And you don't think it's him in there now?'

Jacinta began to feel calmer. She shook her head and a tentative smile lifted her lips. *Fancy being so stupid to think it was Ryder.*

'No way it would be. Ryder was in medical research; he was even talking about applying for medicine when we were going out. But he was worried about the time he'd spend at uni because he often cared for his mum. She was in a wheelchair when I met her; she seemed like a lovely person. Then again, so did he.'

'So, it got as far as meeting his mother?' Bec looked surprised.

'It did. The second time I met him he was with his mother. He seemed so kind and patient with her. That was what really made me take notice of him. More fool me.'

Bec shook her head. 'You've had one bad experience, and you've let it take over your life.'

'I know. Time to pull up my big girl panties, I think. But you know what, Bec? I'm happy with my life. I don't need a man in it. I guess I'm destined to be alone, and I don't mind that one bit.'

'No, Jace. I think we need to find a local guy for you. Maybe we'll get Jules on the job for both of us.' Bec chuckled. 'Sure to be two cowboys out there with our names on them.'

'Cowboys? There're no cowboys in Augathella.'

'Okay, a couple of ringers, then.'

Jacinta knew she was teasing. 'Maybe we do need to go looking,' she agreed with a smile.

'So, are you okay to come back inside? The girls will wonder where we are. Apparently, there's a big set of acrobatics and dancing after the break. They're really good, and it's a professional show.' Bec gestured over to the truck parked at the side of the pub. 'They even have a semi-trailer to bring all their gear.'

Jacinta cocked her head; she couldn't hear any music. 'Are they on a break now? They didn't go for very long.'

'That was the warm-up before the show apparently. To wind the crowd up, and boy, are they wound up. You really have to come back in. Seeing the locals in action is more fun than watching the guys! I'll never look at Jennifer Shaw again without thinking of her with her hand up. "Pick me, pick me!"' Bec giggled. 'Sorry, I'm being a bit of a cow.'

'She's always been a strange one,' Jacinta said.

'So, are you coming back?' Bec stood up and waited for Jacinta.

'I will in a minute, but can you do me a favour first?'

'Sure. Do you want a drink?'

'No, I'll grab one when I'm back inside. Just so I'm completely sure, will you go in there and find out the names of the guys, especially the one who was in the middle with the dark hair? The cowboy with the red and black checked shirt.'

'Sure, there'll be a program somewhere with their names on it. I'll be back in a minute.'

Jacinta closed her eyes. There was no way Ryder would be out here as part of a show like that. Her meltdown seemed embarrassing and over the top now. At least she knew she could trust Bec not to tell anyone how silly she'd been.

I really do need to get a life.

Like Bec said, maybe she needed to look for a local "cowboy". A smile tipped Jacinta's lips as she thought about how happy most of her friends were in relationships. Yes, she'd try and get out more. Time to start living a proper life.

Callie and Braden were married now, and although everyone had been so disappointed that there hadn't been a big wedding, seeing how happy they were more than made up for the lack of a party. From the look of all the planning that was going on, Sophie and Kent's wedding was going to make up for it.

Maybe I'll catch the bouquet.

Huh!

Fallon and Jon were settled and happy with cute little Ryan, and Ben and Amelia had just moved in together. The one romance in town that everyone was watching closely was Dr Harry and Braden's sister-in-law, Laura. They were very hard to pick, but Jacinta had seen them holding hands one night as they walked back to the hospital. Everyone was hoping if they did get together that they would stay in town. Dr Harry had only been here for a short while, but the community loved him. Lots of happy couples and new families were being established.

Maybe I wasted too much time trying to get over Ryder.

She'd trusted too easily and given her heart too quickly. But God, how she'd loved him. She'd loved every minute she'd spent with him, and every moment they'd talked when they weren't together. He had seemed so perfect, and the sad part was, he'd pretended he felt the same way about her. And that's where her judgement sucked big time. She'd believed what she wanted to see. Not the reality, and she honestly didn't know if she was any better these days at picking people. She hadn't quite told Bec the truth. That one night she and Ryder had spent together had been perfect. It was like the stuff of dreams.

And to this day, she still dreamed about that night.

The door opened and Bec came out. 'I brought you a drink too.' She put a glass of bubbles on the table, and her eyes were intent on Jacinta.

'So, any luck with a program? Ease my crazy fears.'

'Okay.' Bec counted the names off her fingers. 'There's Chappo, Hilly, Slim, McPhee and Francesco on the program.'

'What?' Jacinta stared at Bec. 'Did I hear right? Did you say *Francesco*?'

'He's the cowboy.'

As Jacinta jumped to her feet, her drink tipped over, but she ignored it.

Bec leaned forward. 'I'm guessing that's the name you didn't want to hear.'

'It can't be him. Why would he be here?' Jacinta put her hands over her face and her words were muffled through her fingers. 'It's the right name and he looks like Ryder. What the heck is he doing? Maybe he wasn't really a medical researcher, maybe that was all a lie too.' She moved her hands to each side of her head. 'Oh God. I'm out of here, Bec. I don't want to see him. Not tonight, not ever. And I sure don't want to see him cavorting semi-naked in front of an audience of women. *Augathella* women. If anyone ever finds out I went out with him for a while, how can I teach their children? My reputation will be shot. Can you just let Sophie know I'm not feeling well? I'll walk home.'

'Calm down, Jacinta. You're overreacting. No one's going to find out, and if they did, no one would judge you. Everyone knows the real you. You are revered by the community. I often hear how you're the best teacher in the school.' Bec reached over and gently moved Jacinta's hands down from her face. 'Do you want me to walk you home, sweetie? I don't care if I don't go back in there.'

'No, but thanks. Sophie will be upset. I feel bad enough leaving, for her sake. I'll be fine. To be honest I only came because Sophie insisted. It's not my thing. I'd rather be home watching Netflix or reading a book.' Jacinta was making a mammoth effort to speak normally as her head spun and her heart tapped out an erratic beat.

'Okay. I'll call in tomorrow. You're sure you're okay to walk home? You'll be okay?'

'Nowhere safer than Augathella.' She managed to keep her voice calm as she reached over and righted the glass.

'Okay, take care.' Bec waved as she headed back to the pub. 'I'll see you in the morning before I go to work.'

No matter what she'd said to Bec, and what she told herself, Jacinta had never gotten over Ryder. Or the person she'd believed he was. She was a fool, but no matter how hard she'd tried, she couldn't forget him That one night together had firmed her love into the very depths of her heart and soul.

Maybe seeing the *real* Ryder would help her on a path to healing?

Closing her eyes, Jacinta leaned back against the seat. She'd take a few minutes to calm down a little more and walk home. Her heart had slowed but it felt like it was lodged in her throat. She actually felt ill.

Why on earth was he here? Why out of all the small towns in Queensland did Ryder Francesco have to turn up here and ruin her life all over again? Surely he hadn't come here because he thought she was here?

Jacinta shook her head in disbelief.

A male stripper?

What had happened to his medical career?

Or had that been a lie too?

Chapter 3

Ryder

'I thought it was supposed to be stinking hot in the outback?'

Ryder tensed at Bram's whining voice. He turned and shut the window of the small room they'd been given at the back of the pub. It stopped the cold breeze, but the room seemed to get stuffy instantly.

'What the hell is this place anyway? Where are our drinks? Where's the bathroom?' Bram's voice filled the small space as the pub manager who'd shown them there disappeared quickly down the corridor.

'It's fine. We've seen worse, and we'll see a lot worse by the end of the tour,' Ryder said. 'It's all right. I'll go and get some water, and a beer for you. Just focus on the show. We'll have a bathroom in our rooms upstairs. I've got the keys. For the time being, use the bathroom up the hall.'

When Ryder came back with a six-pack and a

jug of water, the costumes for the main show were draped over the chairs and on the table; there was barely enough standing room for the dancers and the crew. The warm-up set was about to begin, and Bram was still in his civvies.

'Get dressed, Bram. You're on in five.' Clive, the manager turned to Ryder. 'Soundcheck?'

Ryder nodded. 'All set.'

'Thanks, can you go down to the bar and say we're right to go in ten? Gives the punters time for one more drink before we hit the stage.'

Minutes later, Ryder closed his eyes as the smoke filled the stage and the music blared out. The screams got louder, and they launched into the ever-popular *YMCA*. By the time they'd started the second song, most of the women were on their feet dancing along with them.

A responsive crowd, Ryder thought, wondering how many entertainers got this far out west. It sure was a long way from the city.

The crowd protested when the music stopped after two songs and the dancers left the makeshift stage.

It only took a minute or so before costumes were draped on every available surface as they got ready for the next set.

'I'm going out to get a breath of fresh air.' Ryder reached for the red and black checked shirt he'd hung on the hook behind the door. 'It's cold out there. You right, Bram?'

'I am. Leave me alone. I'm going to take a leak.'

Ryder glanced at Clive and received a slight nod in return.

'I need one too,' Clive said, following Bram to the door. Ryder knew Clive would keep an eye on Bram while he was outside. He couldn't be a nursemaid twenty-four-seven.

'Don't be long, Ryder. We need you in ten.' Hilly, who doubled as stage manager, called out as Ryder shrugged the shirt on and did up the buttons.

'I'll be quick. Just need a five-minute breather.'

'Okay,' Hilly said as he headed out to the bar. 'Who else wants a drink?'

'I'll have a scotch, please,' Ryder said. 'Put it on the table for me. I won't be long.'

He eased the door open, taking a careful look that no one was hanging around the corridor of the old pub.

He was so over these gigs. Every town was the same. Bored housewives and single women on the lookout for a man, coming along for their night of fun. Ryder hated every minute of it.

As he headed along the corridor, he kept his eyes on the door to the bar area where the stage was set up. No one came out and he slipped through the back door into the cool, sweet air.

Even though the pub was in the centre of town, he could still hear cows lowing in the distance. Looking up, he stared at the myriad of stars sprinkled in the sky above. Moonlight illuminated the flat outback landscape. It was one of the few advantages of being out in the bush; the sky made him feel better at night. Nights like this reminded him of Jacinta. She'd always said she missed the stars when she was in the city, and each night in every town when he looked up at the huge expanse of outback sky, he thought of her, wondering where she'd ended up teaching. She'd come from out this way somewhere, but he couldn't remember the name of the town. He remembered her talking to Mum about the World War II secret base and he knew that was only an hour or so away from where they were.

Since Mum had passed two years ago, his life had changed dramatically.

Overnight.

The promise she'd extracted from him as she lay in Princess Alexandra Hospital gripping his hand would stay with him for the rest of his life.

It had changed his *life*. He'd tried his best, but staying in Brisbane hadn't worked. No matter what he did, everything had gone to shit.

The only way to keep his promise to her had been to head bush; out here in the remote outback, everything had stayed on track.

So far.

But he knew it was only a matter of time.

When he found the dance troupe, it had been the answer to his problems and the past two years had enabled him to keep that promise. It had worked, even though there had been half a dozen or so setbacks in various towns on the way.

Every few months he got a message from Larry, the head of the laboratory, begging him to come back.

He answered the first few messages, but now he ignored them.

The most recent one had hit his phone yesterday afternoon as they drove into Augathella. At least there was phone service in this town. In other small towns out here on the tour there'd been no service, and they'd had to wait for a larger town before they could check their messages. Not that Ryder had any messages to check; Larry was the only one who texted him these days and all that did was fill him with frustration. But the isolation had one big benefit, and it meant his promise had been kept.

Hope all is well with you, mate. Have you given any thought to coming back? We really need

you.

Sissy is pregnant and Darren and Bella have decided to go overseas. I am in dire need of my best researcher. I need you back, Ryder. Please give me a call as soon as you can.

Ryder stopped reading and the despair settled deep in his chest. How much longer could he do this? He knew he was on the verge of depression; he'd love to go back and work at the institute. He couldn't spend the rest of his life traipsing around the Queensland outback, staying in pubs. What a bloody waste of his degree and his years of study. And if he stayed away much longer, he'd be right out of touch with the research. But it appeared Larry believed he still had the knowledge he needed.

We're at a critical point in the research and you know what we were trying to get to. We're so close, mate, and you know what a difference our project findings will make. If we are successful. I really need you here. Please, Ryder, please come back. The salary package I've been authorised to offer you will be like nothing you've ever seen.

Now outside yet another pub, Ryder sighed as he recalled the message.

He didn't care about the money or the salary package. He'd go back and continue working at the institute for the love of his job and the importance of the research he'd been involved in.

But he was bloody stuck.

It was all about the promise he'd made to Mum on her deathbed. The promise that had destroyed his right to have a life of his own. He couldn't break it.

Very rarely did he let himself think about Jacinta. Sometimes it seemed like that first and last glorious night together was only yesterday. Most times it seemed like the years it had been.

Jacinta hadn't even woken when the text from the hospital had come in on his phone. He'd left her apartment expecting to come back to her later that day. When he closed his eyes, he could still see her lying in the bed, her dark hair spread on the white pillowcase, her lips tilted in a gentle smile as she slept.

It was the first time they slept together. It was

the last time he'd seen her.

Now that he was in the west where she'd grown up on a cattle station, Ryder looked for Jacinta in every town they passed through. Stupid, because he knew she'd be working in Brisbane. And doubly stupid, because even if he had seen her, he would have walked away. She was the last person he ever wanted to see again because he knew she was the one person who could make him break his promise to Mum.

Jacinta had shared her plans with him; her plans to work in a city school, and to buy a house on the bay when she'd saved up enough. She wanted to become an assistant principal where she could make a difference—not only in students' lives as far as their education—but to be a decision-making member of the executive team. He admired Jacinta for her goals, her ethics, and the way she wanted to make a difference in children's lives.

He'd fallen hard for her, and Ryder had let himself dream that he'd finally found the woman he wanted to spend the rest of his life with. She was kind and gentle, and he'd fallen in love with her a little more every time he saw her.

But he'd gone slowly; Ryder wanted to be sure, and their times together had been dreamy and romantic.

Regret pierced his heart so hard it was physical pain.

He knew he had broken her heart, and not going back to see her the day Mum had passed, to tell her what had happened, had been the hardest thing Ryder had ever done.

It had been as tough as sitting beside Mum as she drew her last breath. Her eyes had opened for the last time as she smiled up at him and he knew there was no way he would let her down. He held her thin hands, her skin cold and waxy, and a sob rose in his throat as he realised how frail she was. Her rings were loose on her finger and he turned them around so her engagement ring was facing the right way. When he looked back at her beautiful face, she had gone. He stood and leaned over and kissed her cheek.

'I won't let you down, Mum,' he whispered. 'I promise.'

He had to let Jacinta down instead. Maybe he should have gone to see her, to tell her what had happened, but he couldn't bring himself to do it. By the time the funeral was over, it was too late. Too much time had passed, and he had a promise to keep.

His brother hadn't even come to Mum's funeral, and Ryder spent the next week looking for him even though his head and his heart were full of Jacinta.

It had taken a fortnight but he'd found him and every day since then he'd kept his promise.

Even though he hated every second of every day and it had broken his heart.

Moving into the darkness, further away from the hotel, he felt something slip down the front shirt pocket. He reached in and pulled out a small bag of dried leaves.

Bloody Bram had put it in the shirt pocket.

But at least it was only dope.

As he slowly walked towards the two tables on

the far side of the yard, he noticed someone was already sitting at the one furthest from the pub.

Bloody hell.

Hopefully, it wasn't one of the women from inside, but chances were it was.

Ryder didn't want to talk to anyone, but he didn't want to go back inside yet either. That room was claustrophobic, and the way he was feeling tonight, it would bring him undone if he went back in there now. He had to dig deep for strength.

So, he put his head down and walked to the empty table.

A harsh drawn-in gasp stopped him in his tracks.

'Ryder?'

No. no.

His heart skittered to a stop, and then pounded in his chest.

Had he conjured Jacinta by simply thinking about her? He'd know her voice anywhere.

Turning slowly, he faced the woman he loved.

Her dark hair shone in the faint moonlight, but

her face was in the shadows.

'Jacinta?' he said slowly.

'Hello, Ryder. It's been a long time.'

His world spun.

Chapter 4

Brisbane, two and a half years earlier.

Jacinta took to university like a duck to water.

She loved the academic study; she loved the lectures and tutorials, and she really enjoyed her practicums at the local primary schools. She knew that her choice of a teaching career had been the right one all along. Her anticipation to get appointed to a school and put into practice everything she'd learned was keen.

She laughed to herself as she sat on a bench seat near the Brisbane River. It was Saturday afternoon and she took time off her studies every weekend to go and sit at South Bank. Sometimes she dipped her toes in the water of the pool, and sometimes she just sat by the river watching the crowds go by, and enjoyed being in a big city.

Jacinta had planned not to go back to the west of Queensland after she graduated. She'd outgrown

Augathella. The family station was Kent's life now, and she wasn't needed there.

She loved the buzz of the city and she loved the shopping. Watching people, and eating out in different restaurants with the friends she'd made had been a different experience from dinner in the bistro of the pub at home. Most Saturday nights she went out for dinner; it was the one treat she allowed herself. She'd experienced a variety of cuisines in city restaurants and had enrolled in some cooking classes.

Tonight, she was going to a little restaurant in Paddington with Rosie and Sarah, two of the friends she'd made in her first year.

Rosie and Sarah were country girls too, but they were keen to get back to their local communities.

'It's really hard to get teachers out in our town,' Rosie said. 'I'm sure we won't have any problem getting a job, even if it's just relief work to start with.'

Sarah nudged Rosie. 'You only want to go back because you've got a boyfriend in town.'

'What about you, Jacinta? Are you still keen to stay in Brissie?'

'I am. I'm not going back to Augathella,' she replied. 'I love this city. There is so much work, and more opportunities in schools, plus I love living here. I'm going to work for a few years, and I'll save up and buy myself a nice little house down on the bay. Maybe Redcliffe. I like being near the water.'

'You *are* turning into a city girl,' Rosie said. 'There's not much of the country left in you.'

'I bet you haven't been to a Teppanyaki restaurant yet, though,' Sarah said as they waited for a taxi later that night.

'No, this is another first for me,' she replied.

As they sat at the table in the Japanese restaurant, Sarah nudged Jacinta. 'Now there's a looker for you.'

Jacinta looked around to where Sarah had gestured. 'Very easy on the eye,' she said with a smile. 'Movie star looks.'

The barman looked up and saw them all staring

at him. His smile widened and he turned his attention back to the customers waiting to be served.

'Not up himself, either,' Rosie said.

'Used to it, I'd say.' Jacinta smiled. He was a looker though.

'There you go, Jacinta. I wonder if he's available.'

'Cute name too,' Sarah said. 'Ryder.'

'How do you know his name?' Jacinta asked suspiciously. This pair were always trying to set her up.

'Duh, I read his name tag.' Sarah nudged her. 'Stick with me, girl. I'll show you how it's done.'

'Fair enough,' Jacinta shook her head as she chuckled. 'Look, you know I'm not in the running for a man at the moment, thank you very much. I've got my hands full with my study. Don't forget our final exams are only two months away, girls.'

'Final exams, pfft!' Rosie said. 'You're already going to graduate with honours. Jacinta, you're at the top of every subject.'

'What will you do after the exams? Will you go home for a while?' Sarah asked.

Jacinta shook her head. 'No, I don't need to. Kent, my brother, has taken over the station from Dad and he's got it well under control. They don't need me out there, and to be honest, there's not a lot I can do. Even though I grew up on the station, it's not something I enjoy. Kent always said he was born with the cattle in his blood, and I was born with shopping in mine.'

'How do your parents feel about that?' Rosie asked. 'Mine would be devastated. They're waiting for me to find myself a cow cocky and bring him home because I'm the only child.'

'And she's found one,' Sarah whispered loudly.

Jacinta grinned. She knew Rosie was smitten with her Drew, and she expected to be invited to an engagement party any day. 'Mum and Dad are fine with my decision. We've talked about it a lot since I've come back home. They let us each make our own choices. Kent's got a girlfriend and it's pretty serious. I think he and Sophie will be engaged sooner than later. I'll go home for that.'

'We'll be gone and lectures will be done in a couple of months. What will you do in Brisbane by yourself?' Sarah asked.

'I'm going to stay here, and when we finish up, I'm going to have a holiday. I might even go down to the Gold Coast.'

'Wow, very adventurous,' Sarah said with a laugh. She and Rosie were heading off to England for a month; they'd invited Jacinta to travel with them but she'd said thank you, but no.

She couldn't really afford it, money was tight; Mum and Dad had paid for her rent and her tuition, and she intended to pay them back when she started work.

'And I might even get a part-time job, to fill in the days,' she said.

'There's a couple of jobs going here,' Ryder, the good-looking barman said as he stood behind her with an iPad ready to take their orders.

Heat ran up Jacinta's cheeks as she looked up at the guy standing close to her with an expectant expression.

'Um, are we ready to order, girls?' she managed to choke out as self-consciousness flooded through her.

He was even better-looking close-up, and his voice was as sexy as hell. Blue eyes surrounded by long thick eyelashes held hers. 'Would you like more time?'

Jacinta looked at Sarah and Rosie, and then back at him. It was a relief to not look away for a few seconds. She shook her head. 'How about we leave the order in your capable hands'—she glanced at the name tag as if she hadn't already taken note of his name— 'Ryder? We're all inexperienced.'

His eyebrows rose as he held her eyes with those baby blues. 'Inexperienced?'

Sarah and Rosie burst out laughing as he flirted with Jacinta.

'One of us is anyway,' Rosie chortled, and Jacinta's face burned.

'With this sort of menu, I meant.'

His grin was wide and she couldn't ignore the

wink he gave her as he left their table.

As the night continued in the same vein, with Ryder ordering their meals, keeping the drinks coming and managing to flirt with Jacinta each time he came over to the table, she had a good time once her embarrassment fled, and she played along with a bit of harmless fun.

He brought the dessert menu over and Jacinta, who was feeling a bit more confident, glanced through it. 'These don't sound very Japanese to me.'

Ryder cleared his throat. 'Our dessert chef is on holidays, so we only have the ice creams that go with the usual desserts.'

'Ice cream isn't a problem at all, is it, Jacinta?' Rosie said.

The three girls with a few wines in them giggled.

'What's your favourite food, Jacinta?'

'Ice cream helps me study,' she explained.

After they paid the bill at the end of the night, Ryder walked them to the door. 'Can I call you a taxi, ladies?'

'Yes, please. We'll share,' Jacinta replied.

'And don't forget we've got vacancies if you're seriously looking for a job . . .' He winked at her again as the taxi tooted outside.

When they got into the taxi, Sarah and Rosie looked at her as Jacinta put one hand on her chest.

'Be still my beating heart.'

'Did you get his number?' Rosie asked.

'No, but I know where he works,' Jacinta giggled.

Chapter 5

The next morning

Jacinta sat on the brick wall looking over at the brown Brisbane River. Spring was in full bloom and the soft breeze carried the beautiful fragrance of all the spring flowers in the gardens. She put her head back and closed her eyes as contentment slipped through her. Last night had been late, and she was tired after having dinner with Rosie and Sarah, but it had been a fun night. They'd sat there for ages and all three of them had ogled that gorgeous-looking barman as Rosie and Sarah had encouraged Jacinta to interact with him.

But she was shy and she had no time for that sort of thing because she was focused on the last months of her study.

Although she had to admit to herself, he had been *very* easy on the eye. She could still see his face when she closed her eyes. His manners and service had been impeccable; he'd been polite and very kind every time she got up to order a drink for the girls. He'd smiled as she'd ordered soda water for herself after they'd finished dinner and moved on to the delectable desserts. She'd continued drinking soda water for the second half of the evening and watched him as he moved around the restaurant.

Today, she'd given herself a day off from study; Jacinta knew she deserved, and needed a break. The beautiful spring morning had enticed her from her rented apartment and she breathed in the fresh air as she walked along the river path.

Conversations wafted around her as tourists and locals enjoying the beautiful day. A river cat slid silently past as it went up the river towards Kangaroo Point, and she smiled as she saw the children in the front pointing excitedly at the water.

Maybe they were kids like her. Kids from the country who'd never seen a boat on the river or the ocean.

Since she'd arrived in Brisbane Jacinta usually left one day free every weekend to see the sights.

As a child, they hadn't had time for many holidays and the city was a novelty to her. Mum and Dad had been too busy on the property; she and Kent had had one holiday to Yeppoon when they were in primary school and all she could remember was the unpleasant smell of the beach from the coral spawn.

Jacinta much preferred the wide-open spaces of the west and at times, her homesickness made her rethink her decision to stay in Brisbane where she was keen to get a teaching position. It was only that she was tired that she was having doubts, she told herself sternly.

Voices reached her as a man approached pushing a wheelchair.

As Jacinta watched, he stopped, leaned over and smiled at the elderly woman as he spoke to her. She smiled up at him and the love in her eyes was obvious.

Jacinta's heart skipped and she stared as she realised it was Ryder from the restaurant last night. She went to speak and then stopped, not wanting to interrupt such a lovely moment, and then she told herself she had no reason to greet him. She didn't even know Ryder, apart from a fleeting encounter in a restaurant. He probably treated all of the single women as pleasantly as he had treated her. It was his job.

He'd simply been doing what he was paid to do.

He started wheeling the woman again and, feeling foolish, Jacinta sat back waiting for them to pass, but as they approached, Ryder looked over and noticed her sitting there.

He stopped the wheelchair in the middle of the path. 'Hello there.'

Heat ran up her neck as she smiled back. 'Good morning.'

'Hello, dear. Isn't it a lovely day to be out in the sunshine?' the woman said.

'Yes, it sure is,' Jacinta said. 'I love spring and I have decided I particularly love spring in Brisbane.'

'Did you have a nice night last night?' Ryder asked.

Jacinta nodded. 'I did, thank you.'

The woman looked curiously at them. 'Ryder,

please introduce me to this lovely young lady.'

'I would, but unfortunately, I don't know her name.' His eyes crinkled as he tipped his head to the side and looked at Jacinta. 'I looked after this *lovely young lady* and her two friends at the restaurant last night.'

'Oh, I forgot you were still working there,' she said, her lips set in obvious disapproval.

Jacinta looked from one to the other; the woman had to be Ryder's mother. As she watched, he reached out and put the brake on the wheelchair. He held his hand out to Jacinta.

'Hello again, my name is Ryder Francesco and you are?'

Jacinta almost stumbled over her words as she took her hand. He held her fingers, his hand smooth and warm. 'I'm Jacinta Mason.'

The smile stayed on his face and reached his eyes as laughter lines fanned out from the corners. 'This is my mother, Beryl.'

'Hello, Jacinta, it's very nice to meet someone who enjoys the river as we do. Do you live nearby?'

'I live over at Kangaroo Point. I'm renting there while I go to university. I find it easy to get around on the river because I don't have to have a car. I often come and sit here at South Bank. I love watching the crowds. It's very different to what I know.'

'And what would that be?' Beryl asked. 'You're not a Brisbane girl?'

'No, I come from a little town out west. You probably haven't heard of it.'

'Try me,' Beryl said with a cheeky grin.

'Mum was a geography teacher,' Ryder chipped in.

'Augathella,' Jacinta replied, feeling self-conscious as Ryder's eyes didn't leave hers.

'I visited there many years ago,' Beryl said. 'Not far from Charleville, is it?'

'That's right. I was out at Charleville when I was a teenager. My dad worked at the top secret US air force base.'

'Top secret then,' Jacinta said. 'But a huge tourist draw card now. Have you been there?'

'No. It's difficult for me to get around these days, love.'

Ryder stood back as Jacinta chatted to his mum. Jacinta glanced at him occasionally, worrying that she was intruding on their time together, but his expression was relaxed and he looked as happy as he had last night.

'Would you like to walk with us, Jacinta?' Beryl asked. 'We're on our way to have ice cream near the Ferris wheel.'

'Oh, you don't want me to impose on your time together,' she said.

'Of course, I do,' Beryl said. 'I might get more conversation from you than my quiet son.' She reached up and patted his arm where he was holding onto the handles of the wheelchair.

'Only because I can't get a word in, Mum.' Ryder grinned at Jacinta and her tummy did a little flip. He was very good-looking and seemed like a great guy. Much more mature than the guys in her classes at uni.

Beryl laughed at her son. 'Get away with you.'

Again, Jacinta was struck by the easy relationship between them.

'Please do join us,' Ryder said. 'It would be my pleasure to buy you an ice cream. You were all such easy customers last night. Jacinta and her two friends made my night very pleasant, Mum. They caused no trouble and I didn't have to call the police.' He grinned at Jacinta. 'And they left at a reasonable hour.'

'So, you had an early night?' she asked.

'No, after you girls left, that group in the corner across from you decided to party on. They didn't leave until well after midnight. In the end, I had to ask them to pack up because I needed to close up and get home. I knew I'd promised Mum to collect her early.'

'My silly boy works two jobs.' Beryl pursed her lips again. 'He doesn't need to work the job at the restaurant.'

'Mum.' His voice held a warning tone.

'Well, you don't, Ryder.'

She looked up at Jacinta, who was

uncomfortable witnessing the conversation between mother and son.

'Ryder has a very important job in medical research, and he works too hard.' Beryl got the last word in, but Ryder turned to Jacinta.

'Enough of us. Mum and I will never agree. Now, Jacinta, please join us for a stroll and you can tell Mum all about yourself and what you're doing at university and why you love Brisbane so much.' Even though he said she could tell his mum, Jacinta could sense the interest in his eyes.

It felt good, and her confidence increased.

'Thank you, I'd love to join you.' She slipped off the wall and picked up her bag. Walking to the other side of the path, she walked alongside the wheelchair talking to Beryl as Ryder pushed his mother along.

'So university?' Beryl asked.

'Yes. I'm in the final weeks of my teaching degree at UQ.' She glanced up at Ryder. 'With Sarah and Rosie, who were with me last night. They're going to move back home, but I'm hoping to get a job in Brisbane.'

'Ryder went to UQ,' Beryl said.

'I chose it because I wanted to do the special ed. component. They have a very good reputation.'

'So, a teacher?' Ryder commented. 'I can imagine you as a teacher. Primary or high school?'

'Primary, but my special ed. quals overlap into both, so I'll have double the chance of getting the job I want. How long ago were you at UQ?' she asked.

'I graduated three years ago.'

'And like I said,' Beryl interrupted. 'He should be focused on his research job. And shouldn't be working three nights a week at that restaurant.'

Ryder rolled his eyes and winked at Jacinta. She was getting used to that wink.

'Do you enjoy it?' Jacinta asked.

'I do when I get to have excellent customers like I had last night. I spend most of my day in the laboratory by myself and the restaurant stops me from being a recluse. I enjoy getting out and meeting new people and interacting with the world.'

'He doesn't interact with his mother very much. I see him once a week,' Beryl said. 'If he didn't work nights, I might see more of him.'

Ryder's face set into an expression that was hard to read, and Jacinta felt sympathy for him. She was beginning to think her first impression of Beryl had been wrong.

Beryl let out an exaggerated sigh and looked back at her son. 'But I'm well looked after. I have a carer who comes in to look after me and Ryder does ring me every day.'

No one spoke for a while as they reached the end of the path and Ryder turned the wheelchair towards the food court and souvenir shops that lined the path ahead.

'Ice cream,' he announced. 'Let me guess what flavour you'd like, Jacinta.' His grin was boyish.

Jacinta smiled back, challenging him. 'I'll bet you can't guess,' she said.

'I can. Definitely raspberry and white chocolate.'

Her mouth dropped open into an O-shape and

she shook her head. 'You're very clever, Mr Francesco. What sort of research are you in? Mind reading?'

'No, I remember what you chose last night on the main menu so I knew you had a sweet tooth, then you chose white chocolate with dessert, so I'm not so clever after all. Can you guess my flavour?' he asked.

Beryl sat in the wheelchair looking up at both of them, a wide smile on her face as they teased each other.

Jacinta put one finger to her lips and observed him. It was good to be able to look at him without fear of being caught and having a reason to examine him from the top of his head down through that strong face with angled cheekbones, big blue eyes, dark eyelashes and one of the most gorgeous smiles she had ever seen.

'Well,' she said slowly tapping her finger against her lips and a pleasant shiver ran down her back as Ryder's eyes dropped to her lips. 'I guess I would have to say,'—she tapped her finger again and his eyes stayed on her mouth. Her stomach fluttered.

'Come on, I'm waiting to see how good you are,' he said.

Two could flirt. Jacinta held his gaze steadily.

'Oh, I'm good. Very good.'

Beryl chuckled.

'I think you are a no-nonsense chocolate man.'

Beryl's chuckle turned into a full-blown laugh. 'Well, I think you pair are a match made in heaven! He's loved his choccy ice cream since he was a little boy.'

Ryder turned right, pushing the wheelchair across the lawn to a table near the river. He settled Beryl at the end of the table and gestured to the bench on one side for Jacinta to sit down.

'The usual for you, Mum?'

'Yes, please.'

'Now, let me guess what yours would be, Beryl,' Jacinta said as Ryder headed off to the ice cream stand.

'Mine's very simple, love, but I will tell you

because it would be cheating not to. I'll be having a lemonade ice block.'

'You don't like ice cream?'

'Sit down and chat with me. As you can see'—she gestured ruefully to the wheelchair—'I have some health issues. If I look after myself, the days can be okay.'

'I'm sorry to hear that,' Jacinta said.

'Oh, don't be sorry, darling. I have a wonderful life. Children can be difficult at times and I've been well looked after. I had a wonderful husband, but I lost him five years ago. I keep telling Ryder that life flies by and he can't waste it. I get into trouble when I tell him he works way too hard. He doesn't take time out to smell the roses.'

Jacinta smiled. 'I know the feeling. I guess when you were young you were busy too, like we are.'

Beryl nodded. 'In a different way those days. I worked full-time for the first two years we were married and then I stopped working when I had the boys.'

Jacinta waited for her to continue but Beryl didn't mention any other children apart from Ryder and she didn't like to seem curious. They sat there quietly together watching the river flow past. Two dragon boats rowed past with two all-girl crews cheering each other on.

A couple of lone kayakers paddled past and then an outboard boat with four fishing rods in holders puttered by.

'I do love Brisbane,' Jacinta said. 'There's always so much happening and so much to see. If I was sitting on the banks of the Warrego River at home, I'd be lucky to see one cow ambling across the other bank.'

'But that would be very peaceful,' Beryl said. 'Like you, I do love this city. Oh, look. Here comes Ryder now.'

Jacinta watched as he walked across to them. Her mouth dropped open when she saw the triple-serve raspberry and white chocolate cone. 'Goodness me,' she said. 'I'll never eat all of that.'

'I'm sure you will.' He handed it to her and then

unwrapped the ice block for his mother.

They were quiet as they enjoyed their sweet treats and watched the traffic go past on the river. Jacinta surprised herself and managed to finish her ice cream.

Ryan looked at her triumphantly when she held her hands up.

'I need to go find a tap. I'm all sticky. I owe you an ice cream,' she said.

'Same time, same place next week. It's a date,' Ryder said.

Jacinta laughed, unsure whether to believe him or not, wondering if he was just going along with the mood of the moment.

Beryl nodded. 'We'll be here, Jacinta, it's our Sunday afternoon meeting. The only time we can't do it is when Ryder gets called into the Institute on the weekend but that doesn't happen very often, does it, love?'

'No, Mum. I've told Larry, Sunday is my day off, no matter how exciting his discovery or how urgent his need.'

Jacinta went over to the tap, washed her hands and, pulling the handkerchief from her skirt pocket she wiped her fingers.

Beryl's expression was one of delight when she re-joined them.

'Oh my goodness, Ryder, hang onto this lass. A real lady! No awful tissues, she has a handkerchief just like your mother does.'

Jacinta chuckled. 'You sound like my mum, Beryl. She always made sure that we left home with a clean, ironed handkerchief, and I guess I've never lost the habit. My friends can't believe I iron my handkerchiefs and pillowcases. They think it's hilarious.'

'Oh, Ryder, you'll never meet another one like this!'

Beryl was becoming a little too insistent and Jacinta stood, fearing that Ryder was embarrassed.

'It's time I got going. I've been playing hooky from my books all afternoon. It's time for me to go back and study.'

'Another admirable trait, my dear.' Beryl looked

up at her son innocently.

Her insistence that he saw Jacinta again was over the top. Jacinta decided she would make sure she wasn't here next Sunday. Brushing her hands down the front of her skirt, she slipped the handkerchief back into her pocket. 'It's been a pleasure spending time with you both. Thank you for the ice cream, Ryder, and thank you again for looking after us so well last night.'

She turned to leave, but warm fingers gently held her elbow.

'May I walk you to the path?' Ryder asked. He fell into step with her before she answered. 'Please don't let Beryl bother you. I sense that you thought I might have been embarrassed by her comments, but I'm used to her. I just hope she didn't worry you too much.'

'No, not at all, she's a lovely lady.'

'I give her some leeway as she's quite unwell.'

'I'm sorry to hear that.'

'Thank you,' he said. 'It's been an unexpected bonus to have you with us today. Mum really enjoyed your company too. Thank you for being so patient with her and ignoring the fact she was trying to marry us off!'

Jacinta blushed. 'It was good to have some interesting company.'

May I just ask you one thing?'

'You may.' Jacinta looked up and nodded and fell into those blue eyes again.

Ryder held her gaze for a little longer than necessary, and a fluttering took off in her stomach. It had been a long time since a guy had flirted with her.

'May I have your mobile number?'

She couldn't help her smiling nod.

Chapter 6

Callie

Callie walked into the staffroom, a smile tugging at her lips. All the way in from Kilcoy Station, the boys had cracked her up as they practised for their auditions for the eisteddfod.

Rory was a natural; his one-liners and comedic talent were way advanced for an eight-year-old. Nigel, never wanting to be left behind, had tried his best, and poor little Petie had been cackling in the back seat even though he didn't understand half the jokes. He laughed when the other boys laughed. By the time they reached Augathella, Callie was wiping tears from her eyes.

Rory had come out with a one-liner that had absolutely floored her and she couldn't wait to tell Braden tonight.

He told knock-knock jokes all the way and each one had a clever twist. Callie had never heard any of them before. 'Rory, where do you find these?' She glanced at him in the rear-vision mirror and he frowned.

'I make them up. Where else would I get them?'

Callie shook her head and all was quiet for a while.

'Callie?' Nigel leaned forward and his little voice was serious as he said her name quietly. She and Braden had decided that "Callie" would stay; she didn't want the boys calling her Mum—that was Julia's memory for them—although Petie sometimes slipped it out. Braden had agreed, as long as she was happy with that.

I love that man so much, she thought.

Since she had married Braden in a runaway private ceremony in Charleville a couple of months ago, and they had spent the night at the Corones Hotel in Charleville, life had been wonderful.

The boys seemed to have settled a lot and had accepted her as their stepmother; that had been a discussion with them one day. The mornings when the three of them came into their bed for cuddles, and horsey-back rides, and various games, were precious moments.

She loved those boys and she would love and protect them for the rest of her life.

'Callie!' Nigel tapped her shoulder again.

'Sorry, Nige, I was daydreaming. What's up?'

'Did you know there are three types of people: those who can count and those who can't?'

Callie was still grinning when she walked into the staffroom. Coffee was first in order before she went to the classroom and got the room ready for the morning.

As she and the boys stepped out of the warm four-wheel drive, she shivered as the chill wind blew across the car park. The wind had been blowing all night. She and Braden had curled up and watched a movie after she'd finished her lesson prep, and he'd updated his accounts. He'd lit the fire, and it had been romantic. It had been so cold the boys had stayed in their beds until she went in and woke them up when their breakfast was ready. Braden had left at dawn; he was out mustering for two days with Jon Ingram. Callie had offered for Fallon to come and stay, but Fallon had told her that

Ruth had come up for the week.

'She flew over and hired a car. Mum can't stay away from Ryan. I wouldn't be surprised to see them move here,' Fallon said. Seeing Braden wouldn't be home tonight, she and the boys might drive over this afternoon, Callie thought.

Wrapping her hands around the warm coffee mug, she moved across to the window and looked out at the bleak sky, hoping it wouldn't rain while they were out mustering.

When she lived in Brisbane, she'd not been used to the cold; the winters there had always been mild. Even when she'd been a weather girl—gosh, that seemed like a past life now—she'd never taken much notice of the temperatures out west when she'd been doing the forecast for the next day.

On a sunny day without the wind the winter days in the outback were magnificent but today, the cold wind seemed to be blowing straight off the desert.

The door opened and she looked up as Kimberley Riordan, the deputy principal hurried in rubbing her hands together.

Callie grinned at her. 'Coffee?'

'Yes, please. You're in a good mood for a Monday morning, Mrs Cartwright. That's not a Monday morning smile. You must have had a good weekend,' Kimberly said.

Callie moved across to the coffee machine next to the sink and reached for another pod.

'I did. And I'm looking forward to teaching my little darlings today.'

Kimberly gestured to the rest of the room and Callie glanced around at the staff sitting on the seats arranged in a square around a centre table. Conversation was sporadic, and most of the teachers were sitting quietly sipping their coffee, thoughts obviously on the day ahead. It was a great staff, and the communication in the staffroom of a morning was usually lively as they discussed various children and what to be aware of.

'You'd be about the only one,' Kimberly took her coffee off Callie.

'A good dose of Mondayitis?' Callie asked.

'I think everyone's tired after Saturday night. It was a big night in town.'

Callie looked up as Jacinta came into the staffroom, wondering what had been wrong with her on Saturday night. At least it didn't seem like she was sick today.

Jacinta had left almost as soon as the show had started on Saturday night. When Bec had come back inside after checking on her, she had been fairly low-key about what was wrong. Sophie had looked disappointed, but before they could discuss it, the music had started and the second set of the revue had begun. After the show, Callie told Sophie she'd had an enjoyable night. It had been entertaining and even though it wasn't Callie's thing, it had been fun watching the dancing and the acrobatics. But most of their laughter had come from watching some of the usually staid ladies in town as they let their hair down.

She'd never look at Jennifer Shaw in the same way again. Jennifer was sitting quietly over with the other staff, her head down, and her hair hiding her face as she texted on her phone.

Jacinta put her bag in her locker and came over to the coffee machine.

'Good weekend, Jace?' Callie asked as Jacinta reached for a teabag.

'It was okay,' she said.

'You left early on Saturday night.'

Jacinta nodded but didn't explain as she flicked the jug on.

Callie tried to get a smile from her. 'You're going to have fun in your class this morning. Rory is in fine form, so feel free to pull him into line if you have to.'

Jacinta looked at her curiously. 'Why? What's he done?'

'Nothing bad. He's just hyped up. He and Rory have been practising for the eisteddfod all weekend, with Petie and the dogs as their audience. I think when we choose who's going to enter, there's going to be a bit of sibling rivalry there. Rory's the natural but Nigel really wants to be in it too.'

'I can do some work with him today if you like.'

'He needs more than some work,' Callie said with a laugh. 'He needs some better jokes. He delivers everything in a deadpan voice, and most of them aren't terribly funny. Although I have to remember he's only six.'

'No, I meant doing some work on how we can't always have what we want. It can form the theme for our reading session this morning.' Jacinta's voice shook. 'Anyway, if he wants to enter, he probably can. We'll be looking for more kids from our school to enter. I can do some work with him on his jokes and his presentation too.'

Callie glanced across at her. 'Are you okay? You're not your usual happy self.'

'I'll survive,' Jacinta said.

'What's wrong? Look, the sun's come out. Let's go out in the courtyard out of the wind and have a bit of a chat. We've got ten minutes.'

***

Jacinta made her tea and followed Callie across to the sliding glass doors that led to an enclosed courtyard in the middle of the classrooms. It was a well-designed school; each of the four classrooms in this main block took up a quarter of the building and each room had a wet area and a reading area. It was the best school Jacinta had taught in.

Not that she'd been in many other schools—only those where she'd had her prac teaching placements in Brisbane, but Augathella still had one of the best classroom layouts she'd seen.

The primary school had been rebuilt while she and Kent were in high school, and provided a quality learning environment for the students and excellent teaching spaces for the staff. In one way, it took away some of the disappointment of coming back home to Augathella to teach; Jacinta had had her heart set on teaching in the city and making a life and a home there.

But when Ryder had broken her heart, she'd fled home.

Now, her time in Brisbane seemed like a dream.

A lost dream.

Rosie and Sarah were both married now and teaching in Roma and Chinchilla, their home towns, and both regularly invited Jacinta to come and visit.

Apart from attending each of their weddings, she hadn't left Augathella since she'd moved home.

She followed Callie across to the sunny corner. Even though it had rained overnight, the wind had dried the seats. They both sat with their backs against the brick wall cupping their mugs.

'Unusual to have a cardigan on out here,' Callie said, looking at her with concern on her face. 'Are you warm enough?'

Jacinta looked down at her floral skirt and short-sleeved pink T-shirt. 'I'm a local, I'm used to the winters out here. It'll be warm in the classroom. Phil will have turned all the gas heaters on when he cleaned this morning.' As she lifted her mug, Jacinta was surprised to see her hands trembling. It wasn't that cold.

How could a shock stay with you for so long? She'd barely slept for the past two nights, but she thought coming to school would return her to normality.

So, she'd seen Ryder, she'd spoken one

sentence to him, and then he'd walked away.

That should be the end of it. Why was that moment fixed in her mind? She'd done the wrong thing walking away; it made her look like a coward. Maybe she should have stayed and asked him why he'd dumped her.

Maybe she should have stayed and asked him why he was working as a male stripper.

She jumped as Callie's hand touched hers.

'Okay, now tell me what's wrong. You are totally not yourself. Are you sick?'

'No, I'm not sick.' Jacinta stared out over the garden where the courtyard looked over the paddocks.

'So, what's wrong? Are your parents okay? You haven't had bad news, have you?'

'Yeah, Mum and Dad are okay. They're looking forward to coming home for Kent and Sophie's wedding. They're going to look after the station while Kent and Sophie are away on their honeymoon.'

'Is your dad up to that?' Callie knew that Mr

Mason had been ill.

'Yeah. Braden's sending Jon over to Lara Waters for the two weeks to help.'

'Oh yes. I did hear them talking about that.'

Jacinta bit her lip and then turned to Callie. She was a good friend and she knew whatever she told her wouldn't go any further, and it would be good to share. 'Something happened on Saturday night at the pub that I wasn't prepared for.'

'Did someone upset you? It wasn't Jennifer Shaw, was it?'

'No. I did see her on the way in, though. I didn't think that sort of thing would be her scene. Mind you, it wasn't mine either. I suppose the girls thought I left because I was being a prude.'

'No, they were too busy having a good time. Sophie was disappointed, but she got over it. Bec and I were the sober ones and made sure everyone got home safely. So, who upset you?'

Jacinta put her cup down and put her hands over her face. 'I don't know what to do. Or whether I should have acted differently, but I was so shocked,

I just ran away.'

'What happened? You've got me worried. I've never seen you like this.'

'One of the guys in the dance troupe is someone I knew in Brisbane.'

'And he put the hard word on you when you were outside?'

'No.' Her laugh was bitter. 'I probably wouldn't mind that. At least I'd know he still fancied me.'

'Still?'

'Ryder and I went out together for six months just after I'd done my final exams. We were really close—or at least that's what I thought—and I had a whole dream future built in my mind. After he left me, I rejected the job offer I got in Brisbane. I was lucky there was a position out here. That's why I didn't start here until the middle of term one the year I came to Augathella. He walked out on me, Callie. That's why I came back home. No explanation, no nothing. In hindsight, I overreacted. I should have stayed in Brisbane and moved on.'

'Was he a dancer back then? Hang on, did you

say, Ryder? There wasn't a Ryder there.'

'Ryder Francesco.'

Callie nodded. 'Okay. He must use a different stage name. Bram Francesco was the dancer on stage.'

Jacinta shrugged. 'I didn't stay long enough to see. As soon as I saw him come out on stage, I took off. Bec came out and told me his name was on the program.'

'Ryder or Bram?'

'Ryder. He found me out in the beer garden. I thought I'd gotten over him but when I saw him it all came back. I went to pieces. When he walked away, I took off home. I had a shocking day yesterday. I couldn't get him out of my mind. I scrubbed the apartment from top to bottom. Kent and Sophie asked me out for dinner at the pub last night but I said I had schoolwork to do. I was scared the dancers would still be at the pub. And I sat there like an old tragic listening to love songs and crying my eyes out. I'm pathetic.'

'No, you're not. You had a shock. Did you talk

to him? Do you know why he walked out on you?'

'No, he didn't say a word. It was dark but he did look shocked to see me.'

'He didn't know you were out here?'

'We've had no contact since the night he left my . . . my apartment.'

She had almost said "bed".

'What did he say when he left you then?'

'Nothing, one minute we were . . . close, and seeing each other all the time. Talking on the phone every day. And then there was nothing. He just cut all ties. I didn't see him again.'

'Weren't you worried he'd been in an accident or something?'

'I was. But when I finally rang him after a couple of days, he'd changed the message on his phone and I knew he didn't want to see me.'

'What did it say? Was it specifically for you?'

'No. It said just to leave a message as he was very busy with work and he may not get back to the caller, and that he'd be unavailable for a few months. It was so out of character, I figured he just wanted to break it off. The next time I called the number had been disconnected.'

Jacinta gripped her hands together in her lap. 'But you should have seen the shock on his face when he saw me. Callie, he just looked at me and said my name, and I said to him, "It's been a long time, Ryder." He stared and then he turned on his heel and he left me again.'

Jacinta lifted her hands to her face and began to cry.

Chapter 7

Sunday

The show at the pub at Augathella on Saturday night seemed to have gone okay by the audience response, but Ryder didn't care. He'd spent most of the time sitting backstage, letting the stage crew do the work.

Seeing Jacinta in that pub garden had thrown him and he'd just walked away and left her. He couldn't believe he'd done that.

When they went back on stage, he kept scouring the audience even when the lights went out. When the lights came on, he couldn't see her. He thought she must have come up to Augathella for the show but the more he thought about the name of the town, the more it began to ring a bell.

He didn't even know if she'd been at the show. Maybe she had just been sitting out there waiting for someone. Maybe she had a partner who worked at the pub. Maybe she drove a friend to the show, maybe she'd—

Ryder shook his head. All he knew was that he should have shown some common decency and spoken to her instead of walking away.

Somehow, he'd sensed she was nearby and it had been the strangest feeling. She had been in his thoughts all afternoon.

To treat her like that had been cruel and callous. He should have said something like, 'Well, fancy seeing you here,' then talked about the weather, and passed the time of day.

But Ryder knew immediately he spoke to her, he would be lost. He would have put his arms around her, even knowing nothing about her these days. She probably had a partner; a beautiful soul like Jacinta wouldn't have been alone for long. He just wished it could have been him.

But he couldn't risk it; he knew he wouldn't be able to leave her a second time. The first time had broken his heart. If he had spoken to Jacinta last night, he would have risked breaking his promise.

Just after dawn on Sunday, Ryder drifted off into a deep sleep and was woken up soon after by someone pounding on the door.

'Who is it? he yelled.

Clive opened the door and looked around the room before spotting Ryder still in the bed.

'Hey, mate, you okay? Not like you to sleep in.'

'I didn't sleep very well.' Ryder sat up and looked at the empty single bed next to him. 'Shit, what time is it? Where's Bram?'

'Calm down. He's with Hilly; he'll keep an eye on him. They're in the bistro having breakfast. Not that there's anything for you to worry about in this town. You could fire a shotgun down the main street and not hit a single thing, human or animal. It's like a ghost town. But I guess it is Sunday; they're probably all at church. Listen, the chef clears breakfast away in fifteen minutes; that's why I came looking for you. To tell you to hurry up or miss out.'

'Thanks. I'll grab a shower, and be straight down.'

'Listen, we're not booked into Blackall until Tuesday night and the boys have agreed they're quite happy at the pub here, so we've spoken to the manager and we can stay here three nights instead of the one night we booked. Are you okay with that?'

Not really, Ryder thought. The sooner they got out of this town, the better. But he couldn't argue if they'd already booked the extra two nights, plus he couldn't give a good reason for not staying.

He nodded reluctantly. 'Sounds like a plan.'

'Sean, the bistro chef, was telling us there's a shearing show out at one of the properties today and they run a bus out there mid-morning. It was only half-full, so he said he can fit us all in. The boys thought they'd like to go out, especially Bram. He said if he's a cowboy he needs to know about what's happening out here to make his performance authentic.'

Ryder rolled his eyes. 'Typical. It's all about Bram, isn't it? The centre of attention as usual.'

Clive looked at him carefully as Ryder climbed

out of bed. 'He's been going really well, mate. You're doing a fine job.'

'Yeah, but for how long, Clive? How long till he gets his hands on something again?'

'Nowhere out here, Ryder. He doesn't know anyone, and I've been keeping a very close eye on him too.'

'I appreciate it, mate.'

And he did appreciate it. When they'd both been hired by the dance troupe and met Clive, Ryder had known straight away he had an ally. A straight shooter, and not scared to say what he thought, Clive had pulled Bram up a few times so far on the tour.

'You have to trust him more, Ryder. He's trying his best. He wants to do it and with support, he'll get there. And he's by far the best performer in the troupe. You know he could make a career without these guys.'

Ryder ran a hand over his hair. He was way overdue for a haircut. God knows what Jacinta had thought of him last night; unkempt hair and in a flanny shirt, looking like a dropkick.

'I know. I didn't tell you—or Bram—that I was approached by a TV network guy from Sydney when we were in Cairns. He was going to offer him a job on one of those celebrity dance shows.'

Clive looked at him quizzically. 'You don't think you should have run it by him before you said no?'

Ryder shrugged. 'How would I nursemaid him in the centre of a city? A city I don't know.'

'You just gotta have faith, mate. It'll happen one day. You're not going to have to play nursemaid for the rest of your life.'

'Do you really think that?' Ryder said. 'I know my brother better than you do, Clive, and I can't see this clean streak lasting.'

Clive shrugged, but he looked sympathetic. 'Are you going to come out to the shearing demo on the bus with the rest of the boys? And you better skip that shower or you'll miss breakfast.'

'No, tell them I'm not coming down. I think I'll hang around town for a while. I'm sure I'll be able to get a coffee somewhere. Sit in the sun and have a bit of a rest, read some articles.'

'Sounds exciting. Reading medical journals.'

Ryder nodded. 'That's me. The exciting life of Ryder Francesco in the outback.'

Clive looked at him for a long moment and shut the door as he left the room.

##

Ryder walked the streets of Augathella, and that didn't take too long. Even on a bleak winter's day, he could see what a graceful old town it was. The occasional locals he passed, mowing their lawns or sitting on their porches, waved and greeted him as he walked past. For a while, walking pulled him out of his dark thoughts.

Once he got back into the main part of town, Ryder stood in front of the cinema for a long time looking at the painting of the character on the front of the old timber building. Dad had called him

Smiley when he'd been a little tacker, and he'd said it had been from a movie he'd seen when *he* was a kid.

According to the sign painted on the timber building in 2008 celebrating the fiftieth anniversary of the movie, Smiley Creevey had been an Augathella local and had passed away a long time ago.

Dad had passed away when Ryder and Bram were at high school, and sometimes he thought that had a lot to do with Bram going off the rails. Mum had had no idea of how to deal with a rebellious teenager.

He headed back to the pub after walking for a couple of hours and seeing no sign of Jacinta. For a minute, he even doubted himself. Had he imagined the whole thing last night?

Had it really been Jacinta?

Yes, it had been her. She'd called him by name.

Feeling a little more settled after his walk, Ryder headed back to the pub. He'd have some lunch and nurse a beer and watch the world go by.

Never give up hope, he thought to himself. Even if he did see Jacinta, what could he say?

He knew what he wanted, but she wouldn't think much of him now; not after he'd left her with no explanation. And even if by some miracle she did still care for him—because he knew they'd had something special together two years ago—he wouldn't start a relationship again.

But he *had* to see her. He couldn't stay in her town, and not make the effort.

If he could just see her briefly and make his peace, and explain why he hadn't contacted her.

Things had been critical the morning he'd left. Mum, and Bram. If he could tell Jacinta how bad things had been and why he'd had to leave, she might forgive him.

Maybe Bram would get better and Ryder could go back to his old life. The life he missed every single day.

But even if he went back to his research job, there'd be no chance of going back to Jacinta. She had chosen to come and live back out in the west, and his future was in Brisbane.

Not that she'd want you anyway, he thought.

Things were improving with Bram, but Ryder couldn't ignore that hard lump of sadness and regret that was lodged in his chest.

He'd lost her forever, but he'd feel better if he got to say goodbye properly.

Tomorrow he'd go and look for her. If he found her, then it would be her choice.

Chapter 8

As he crossed the road to the Augathella hotel, an old guy sitting at the table near the door called out to him. 'G'day mate, the name's Reg. Are you going to have a beer? Come and sit with me and have a yarn.'

'Sounds good,' Ryder replied. 'What are you drinking?'

'A VB would be good, thank you.'

The barman grinned at Ryder when he ordered two VBs. 'Old Reg gotcha, did he?'

'I've got nothing much to do today, so I thought I'd keep the old fella company. He looked lonely.'

The medical articles could wait. He had no idea why he was keeping up to date with the research progress anyway.

'Mate, he has more company out there every day than anyone in town, and he gets most of his drinks bought for him. He's a crafty old bugger, but I'll give him this. He is interesting to talk to.'

Ryder paid for the two middies and took them

outside. While he'd been at the bar, a second chair had appeared at the table.

He sat down and lifted his beer. 'Cheers, mate. I'm Ryder.'

'Nice to meet you. How long are you in town for?'

'Just a couple more days. I've been looking around this morning. Nice place. Brought back some childhood memories.'

'You been here before?'

'No, but my dad used to call me Smiley after that guy painted on the front of the old cinema.'

'My dad knew Didy Creevey,' Reg said. 'That was Smiley's real name. There's a lot of history in this town.'

'You grew up here?'

'I did. I was a shearer until bloody arthritis got to me.'

Ryder swallowed and wondered if he should ask. 'I think some friends of mine have a place out this way. Not sure if they run sheep. Do you know the Masons?'

'Yep, sure do. They've got a big spread southwest of town. Kent's running it these days since old Maso got crook. He's in Brisbane now. Maso, his dad, I mean. You know Kent, do you? He's a top bloke. Couldn't get helicopter pilots for mustering a few years back, so he went and got his pilot's license. Mind you, means he'll be able to take his new wife shopping in the city. He rescued her a few months back.' Reg sighed. 'There's been some hitching in this town lately, so watch out, mate.'

'Hitching?' Ryder asked, looking around for horse rails.

'Weddings, mate.'

'No fear of that for me,' Ryder said, and he half-smiled as his next words sounded lame. 'Does Kent have a sister?' The words forced themselves out.

'Yeah, she's a teacher at the primary school. Jacinta. Nice quiet girl.'

'Does she still live out on the property or is she married?'

'No, she lives in town, down in Nelson Street,

near the old Charleville Road.' Reg narrowed his eyes and looked at him suspiciously. 'Maybe I'm saying too much. You're one of those naked dance guys, aren't you? I'd hate you to go and hassle her.'

Ryder chuckled. 'I'm not a naked dance guy. Did you go to the show last night, Reg?'

Reg spluttered into his beer and froth stuck to the stubble on his cheeks. 'Bloody Nora, no! Why would I want to do that? But I did see all the local women who went in before dark. And then I could hear them yahooing from my place up the street. That just about did my head in. I honestly don't know what this town's come to, inviting trash like that to our old pub.'

He shook his head as he wiped his face with a grubby handkerchief. 'I might sound a bit rude to you, but I'm an old timer. We had standards back in the day. The thought of any man taking his clothes off and dancing to get some women excited is bloody off. Not that I mean you. You seem like a decent enough man. And if you're a friend of Kent's you must be okay.'

Ryder nodded. He didn't know what to say as his thoughts focused on Jacinta.

Reg's voice was droning on in the background and Ryder switched off.

'Well, do you?' the old fellow said loudly.

'Sorry, what did you say?'

Reg put his beer down on the table. 'I said do you know how old the pub is? But a bloke your age probably isn't interested in history.'

Ryder looked up at the building above the tables they were sitting at. A few planter baskets hung crookedly along the edge of timber joists that were bowed with age. The plants in the baskets were obviously last summer's blooms, they were brown and dried. Paper wasps had built a nest on the bottom of two of them.

Reg was watching him.

'It looks old,' Ryder said, wondering if that was the right thing to say when Reg glared at him.

He was a bit over getting judged by this old bloke.

'Let me tell you a bit about the history of

Augathella,' he said.

Ryder sipped on his beer as Reg filled him in on the history of the pub and most of the other buildings in town, but his thoughts were on Jacinta as the old man's voice droned on.

'In 1864, a couple of adventurous souls set up shop on the Warrego River. Sam and Mary were their names and they set up a store. A town sprang up, and it was first called Burenda, and then Ellangowan, like the other pub in town and then it ended up being Augathella. You know what "thella" means? Do you?'

'Ah, sorry. What what means?'

Reg shook his head and looked as though he was debating whether to give Ryder the flick or keep his company in case he got another beer bought for him. He drained his middy and looked down at the empty glass, and then up at Ryder. 'Means waterhole. So, Augathella stuck.'

Ryder went back to his thoughts and tried to keep an interested look on his face.

Single and working at the primary school.

Maybe he'd call in and see if Jacinta would have a coffee with him, and he could apologise to her. Try to explain what he was doing out here.

He knew he wasn't ever going to be at peace with himself until he spoke to her.

God, he'd thought of her every day over the past two years, and regret had stayed with him.

He was going to seek her out now that he knew she worked at the primary school and lived in town. He wouldn't go down that street where Reg said she lived because if she saw him, it would look as though he was trying to find her. A bit like stalking.

Ryder remembered the corner of that road. There was a block of fairly new brick apartments on one side of the road looking out to the paddocks. They were neat and tidy and a lot newer than any of the other buildings. Maybe it was government housing for the workers out here. He'd struck that in other towns. Some of the housing was for the teachers, nurses, and police. Some of them were in compounds and fenced off, but Augathella looked like a quiet peaceful town. He wondered why she lived there instead of on the family farm, but then he realised not every adult lived with their parents.

But he'd struggled with Mum, even living away. Towards the end, she had become querulous, and he had to remind himself she was in pain. Bram had left him to it but had finally come to visit a few days before she passed. He was sure it was the state that Bram was in that had upset their mother and caused her to extract that promise from Ryder.

There had been three cars parked in the carport of the three units so he assumed that one of them was Jacinta's. He wondered if he'd known before that she lived there, whether he would have knocked on her door or walked past.

Ryder's emotions were in such a state, he didn't know what he would have done.

He didn't really know what he was going to do.

Or say.

But there was no point worrying and wondering. All he had to do was go to the school tomorrow and ask to see her, or make an appointment, or leave his phone number.

'So that's a good story, isn't it, mate?'

Ryder looked back at Reg and nodded. 'A very interesting history of the area. I come from Brisbane and I was interested in the history of the settlement of my town, but it's nowhere near as personal as living in a small town like this.'

'Yep, it's a pretty good place. When are you guys moving on and where are you going next?'

'A place called Tambo.'

'I better send them a warning at the pub. I know most of the pubs around here. Then up to Blackall?'

'Yep, we're going there too, and then back down to Charleville.'

'And you gonna catch up with the Masons while you're here?'

'Maybe. Maybe not. I'll see what the day brings,' Ryder said. 'Now can I buy you another beer before I head back to my room?'

'Thought you'd never ask, son. Appreciate your company. I meet some interesting people sitting out here, you know. I've played a bit of Cupid in my time. I've watched all the local romances develop here over the past few months. Gonna have another romance for you too, I reckon.'

Ryder's laugh was grim. 'I don't think so, mate. Like I said, I'm not the marrying type.' He stood and headed for the bar.

As he waited at the bar to be served, their tour van pulled up outside the pub. The automatic doors of the van opened. There was much hilarity and laughter as Hilly, Bram, Slim, McPhee, and Chappo tumbled off the bus, followed by a scowling Clive.

'Just make that another middy for Reg, please, mate,' he asked the barman.

'Looks like they've had a skinful. I can't serve them, you know. The local sarge will have my guts for garters if I do.'

'No problem. I'll go and have a word.'

Ryder carried the beer out to Reg. 'Good talking to you, Reg.'

Bram's eyes were bright and Ryder took a second hurried look, but when he smelled the beer on Bram's breath, relief followed quickly.

'Jeez, Ryder. You should have come. You don't

know what you missed out on,' Bram said, his words spilling over each other as he jigged around. 'Bloody amazing stuff.'

Riley looked at him carefully, waiting to get a word in.

'You should've seen it. This bloke, he sheared about a hundred and fifty sheep in an hour.'

'Really?' Ryder raised his eyebrows. 'Superman?'

'Super Shearer.' Bram cracked up at his own words and Chappo and Hilly laughed with him.

Clive stepped in. 'I think you're exaggerating a bit, Bram. He said, on a good day he might shear a hundred and fifty, but not all the time.'

Bram's eyes were wide, and he reminded Ryder of when he was a kid and had eaten too many sweets. 'And then the lady of the property gave us a cup of tea and some scones and then her husband winked at us. He was a great bloke. He took us out to the shearing shed. The shearers had just knocked off and he had a few beers there.'

'I can see that. Just a few?' Ryder said.

'Yeah, *juss* a couple,' Chappo slurred. 'Homebrew and it was like rocket fuel.'

'Come on, boys,' Hilly said. 'We'll go in the bar and have a couple of beers before dinner.

'I think you'll find you'll be served a soft drink,' Ryder warned. 'Apparently, the local cop's pretty strict.'

Bram stumbled as he walked towards the door. 'Stuff that, then. I'm going to go and have a kip. I'm knackered.'

'Yeah, I might come up with you,' Clive said. 'I've had enough to drink.'

'What about you, Ryder, what have you been doing? Sitting drinking with that old timer all day?'

'Nah, I went for a walk. I might stay down here with the guys and have a yarn about what we're doing this week.' He herded the three of them to a table right in the back corner of the pub and asked the barman for a jug of water on the way past.

Bram and Clive disappeared upstairs, watched closely by Ryder. When he turned back to the table, Reg's eyes were on them. The old bloke certainly didn't miss a trick.

Asking him if he was here for romance! Ryder huffed. The last thing on his mind now, and forever probably.

Hilly turned to Ryder when he pulled out a chair and sat down. 'When we were out at the sheds, I had a bit of an idea I reckon we could come up with a new routine, sort of. I mean, I know we do the cowboy thing in the Village People song. But now we're out west, I reckon we should do something like a sheep shearing thing or something to do with the country. I reckon the ladies'd appreciate it.'

'Not a bad idea.' Ryder nodded slowly.

'We could even get a sheep up on the stage.'

'That's *not* a good idea. You guys talk it out and I'll take a look. We might be able to get something together before Charleville. Apparently, we've sold the most tickets there. I'm sure you can scrounge some western clothes at one of the shops out here, you know the RM Williams-type stuff in the moleskin trousers and the checked shirts.'

Ryder laughed and looked down at his

flannelette shirt. 'Okay, scrap the checked shirt. We already do that.'

The conversation was light as Hilly and the other guys began to sober up. Ryder had gotten chilled sitting outside with Reg, so he treated himself to one rum before dinner. The warm spirit burned its way down his throat and a warm glow inside made him feel a bit happier. As had Bram's decision not to keep drinking.

Bram was going well; the tour was going well, and tickets were sold out at some of the larger towns they were visiting. Ryder didn't have to worry about too much promotion in the west; it seemed as though word of mouth fired up interest.

Looking around the pub he could understand why; it didn't look like there was much entertainment in the small towns.

He wondered what Jacinta did for entertainment. The Queen concert he'd taken her to at the Gold Coast was the first live event she'd ever been to. She'd been blown away by the crowds.

That was the first time he'd kissed her. Ryder

could never hear a Queen song without thinking about that.

Chapter 9

Just before five o'clock, Ryder stood and stretched. The boys had been playing pool and they'd settled down a lot. Clive and Bram hadn't come back down yet.

'I'm going up for a shower, guys,' he said. 'I'll see if we have to book a table for—'

He stopped when Clive hurried into the bar, his face set in a frown.

'Has Bram been down here since I went upstairs?' he asked, looking around.

'No. Why?'

Cliff gestured to Ryder with a quick nod towards the corridor. 'His door's locked and I can't raise him. What do you reckon we should do?'

'Bloody hell, I don't like the sound of that.' Ryder took off for the stairs leading up to the first floor. 'I got a spare key to his room when we checked in; the manager was happy to give me one when I asked.'

'What did you say?'

'Not a lot. I just said he was my brother and he had a few problems and I needed to have access to his room if he locked me out.'

'Fair enough, where's the key?'

'It's up in my room.'

Clive raced up the stairs after him.

'I'll knock on his door again while you get the key.'

Ryder quickly went into his room and got the key from the top of the chest of drawers. By the time he went up the corridor, Clive was knocking on Bram's door again.

'Nothing, mate. I can't hear anything in there. No TV on or anything.'

Rather than barging straight Ryder knocked on the door loudly. 'Bram, it's me. Open the door.'

All was quiet.

Shit.

He put the key in the lock and pushed the door open.

His worst fears were realised.

Bram lay crossways along the bed on his back.

His eyes were wide and glazed, and he looked at them without any sign of recognition.

Ryder raced over and rolled him onto the recovery position. 'Bram, can you hear me? Talk to me.' He looked up at Clive. 'You got your phone handy? We need to call triple zero. And fast.'

'Probably quicker to take him to the hospital in the van.'

'Do you know where the bloody hospital is?' Ryder asked as Bram moaned. He hadn't seen a hospital as he'd walked around the town today.

'No, but I'm sure the guy down in the bar will be able to tell us. You go and ask. I'll make sure he doesn't choke here.'

Ryder took off down the steps and pounded into the bar. Hilly and Chappo looked at him with concern. There was no sign of Slim.

Ryder shook his head as he headed across the bar. 'We've got an emergency. I need an ambulance or the hospital. Which is the quickest, do you reckon?'

'If you don't need the paramedics, you'd

probably be best to go direct to the health centre. We've only got the one ambulance in town and I saw it drive out a while ago.'

'Where is the health centre?'

The barman pointed up the road towards the highway. 'Two blocks, turn left, second right and you'll see the health centre ahead of you.'

'Thanks, mate. Can we use the back door?'

'Sure. Just come down the steps and head down the corridor and bring your car around the back. How about I ring the hospital for you and check that Dr Higgins is there to see you?'

'Appreciate it. Thank you.' Ryder yelled out to Hilly. 'Mate, can you bring the van around the back, pronto?'

He raced up the stairs and into the room. Clive still had Bram on his side; his breathing was shallow.

'Where the hell did he get it?' Ryder said.

'He must've got it out at the farm. He stayed with a couple of blokes while we were having a beer.'

'And here was I, thinking we're so far out in the boondocks, he'd have no chance.'

'You're being a bit unfair, Ryder. You can't blame the town. If he wants it, he'll find it. The only way you can do any more is to put him in a clinic. If he wants to use, he'll always find a way. No matter what he says. You have to accept it, mate. Bram's an addict, and that's not going to go away because we're touring around out here in the outback.'

Between them, they managed to carry Bram down the steps and out the back door. Hilly had the car engine running.

'Shit, what's he gone and done now?' he asked as Clive and Ryder eased Bram into the back of the van.

'Hilly, can you come and hold him with Clive, please? I'll drive.'

The guy from the bar hurried outside as Ryder was heading around the van. 'All good, mate. The doc wasn't there, but they've called him. They said he'll be there by the time you get there.'

'Thanks, I owe you a beer or two.'

'No problem, all part of the territory. You'd be surprised how often I have to do things like this out here.'

Ryder got in the driver's seat, turned the key and then floored the pedal. Two minutes later they pulled up in the emergency bay outside the hospital.

Jesus, is this ever going to end?

He knew the drill. This was the seventh—or was it the eighth time—Bram had ended up in emergency over the past two and a half years?

Bram had come around a little bit and was trying to sit up. Clive and Hilly held him steady as he tried to reach the door.

'Let me out! Friggin' let me out.'

'What did you take and where did you get it?' Ryder's voice was clipped as he turned off the engine.

Clive shook his head. 'Leave him. We've gotta get him sorted first.'

As Ryder opened the door of the van and climbed out, a woman came out the front door accompanied by an orderly with a trolley.

'I'm Nurse Bec Hunter,' she said. 'An overdose?'

That one word was enough to send something skittering down Ryder's spine. Whether it was disgust, impatience, or frustration, he didn't know.

He just knew he was bloody sick and tired of it.

'Looks like it, but we don't know what.'

'Dr Higgins is a couple of minutes away,' Nurse Hunter said. 'We'll get him into emergency. No idea at all?'

'None.' Ryder knew his tone was hard but the emotion of seeing Bram overdose again in a place he'd foolishly thought was safe where he'd stay clean, had hit Ryder squarely in his gut. As they wheeled Bram down the corridor, he thought he was going to throw up.

Clive squeezed his shoulder. 'Calm down, mate.'

Clive had been an absolute godsend and had watched Bram as closely as Ryder had since they'd joined the dance troupe. Clive had put in a good word and got Ryder on the crew. Not that he knew anything about dancing, or sound and technology, but he'd learned a lot since he'd started on the road with the troupe.

Clive had picked Bram's addiction straight up. He'd been a counsellor in a previous career but had lost his job under a restructure. Like Ryder, he'd had a total change of direction, and taken on managing the group.

Three weeks after he'd made his promise to their mother, Ryder had quit his job and was heading for the Atherton Tablelands on the first leg of the tour.

Bram had gotten high a couple of times on dope in those first weeks, but Ryder watched him carefully. He'd stayed clean until they were in Mt Isa.

'Maybe he's been using the whole time and I missed it,' he said to Clive as they headed for the waiting room.

'Stop beating yourself up, mate. It's not your fault. Jesus, Ryder. You've been playing nursemaid to your brother for how long now?'

He sat on one of the plastic chairs and ignored Clive's question. 'As far as I know, he hasn't since we left Mt Isa, but I'm probably way off base.' There had been a couple of nights on the north coast when Bram disappeared at night, but he'd been fine the next morning, so Ryder had relaxed.

He put his elbows on his knees and leaned forward. 'I'm over it. I'm over him. Maybe we should leave.'

Clive's hand settled on Ryder's shoulder. 'Don't make any decisions when you're emotional.'

They sat there quietly for about ten minutes and then Clive nudged him. 'Look, here comes the doctor now.'

'Gidday there,' the tall man with greying hair said. 'I'm Dr Higgins. Harry Higgins. Let's have a bit of a talk.'

Chapter 10

Jacinta - Monday afternoon

Somehow Jacinta managed to get through Monday. Callie had been right; Nigel was off the air and all he'd wanted to do *all day* was tell jokes to the rest of the class.

Jacinta had to pull him into line a couple of times and focus on getting him to behave. Keeping the class on track improved her mood as the day progressed. Thanks to Nigel she was able to focus on the kids and get Ryder out of her head. He would have left town by now and she could forget about him. Mid-afternoon, the children were sitting quietly working with their pencils with Nigel shooting her the odd dirty glare. Jacinta took a deep breath and walked over to the window.

She loved the unique smells of her classroom. Monday mornings, the kids were in clean uniforms and the room smelled fresh. By Friday, with squashed banana sandwiches in some bags, the aroma from the little alcove where the children hung their bags mingled with the smell of paint and crayons.

Phil, the cleaner, managed to air the classroom out at the end of the week and Monday mornings they always came back to a spotless classroom.

The fragrance of the sweet peas Bec had dropped in yesterday to cheer her up wafted across the room. Jacinta had them in a little crystal vase on her desk.

It had been very thoughtful of Bec, knowing how down she was after Saturday night. She'd been to Jenny Riley's place to get the flowers. Jenny's garden was always a picture and apparently, she still had some late sweet peas flowering. Unusual for winter, but having a conservatory, Jenny was always able to supply flowers for town functions.

Bec had been coming over for a coffee on Sunday night, but she'd called to say there was an emergency at the hospital.

'I'll catch you through the week, Jace. Have a good week, and don't brood. Okay?'

'Okay,' she'd agreed.

The sweet peas had brought a smile to her face for a short while. Until she'd spoken to Callie before school this morning, she'd been overwhelmed with the crushing feeling of seeing Ryder again.

Standing looking out at the paddocks across the road from the school, she tried to talk sense to herself as the children worked quietly.

One. She was back in the place where she belonged. She could teach here. She didn't need the city.

Two. She was happy at this school. She had a lovely classroom to work in and her apartment was a pleasant place to live.

Three. She had wonderful, supportive friends.

Four. She had Kent and Sophie's wedding to look forward to, plus Mum and Dad were coming home for a few weeks.

So why did she feel so awful? She hadn't felt that way before Ryder had turned up.

Because she knew she still loved him, and he didn't want her.

'You're just going to have to forget about him all over again. Pull up your big girl panties and appreciate what you have,' she told herself sternly.

'Miss! Miss! Miss Mason!' Nigel Cartwright stood beside her with a strange look on his face.

'What's wrong, Nigel? Have you finished your drawing?'

'No. I just wanted to ask you something really important.'

Jacinta crouched down in front of him and spoke quietly. She was aware of the difficulties that Nigel had been having coping with the loss of his mother, but he'd seemed much improved lately.

'What is it? Is everything okay? Do you need some time out?'

'It's really, really, really important and I really need the right answer. It's…it's… um… I heard a word but I can't remember it. I know, it's life-threatening!'

Jacinta raised her eyebrows. 'Life-threatening? That sounds very serious. You'd better tell me.'

'No. I have to ask you and you have to give me

the right answer.'

'Well, Nigel, as this is such a dire situation, you'd better ask me. I'll do my best. Hit me with your question.'

His little face split into a grin. 'Okay, here goes, Miss.'

Jacinta waited.

Nigel rolled his lips around in a strange grimace and then scratched his head. He lifted one leg and balanced on the other as she waited.

'Nigel, what is it?' she asked.

His face twisted into a horrific grimace and he leaned back. Jacinta got such a fright she reached for him, forgetting she was crouched down and almost fell back on her bottom

'Nigel, what is it? Are you sick? Or do you need to go the toilet?'

'No. I'm just getting myself in the right mood to ask the question,' he said slowly. 'Are you ready now?'

Jacinta started to twig to what he was up to. 'Just ask the question. Say the words in your mind,'

She couldn't help the grin that was tugging at her lips.

'Are you ready?'

'I sure am. The suspense is killing me. Okay, what's your question? It's almost time to pack up.'

His mouth settled in a wide smile. 'Okay, I guess you're ready?'

'I am.'

'Knock, knock.'

'Nigel, how many times today have I told you that we're not practising for the eisteddfod now?'

'But Miss, I finished my drawing and I've done everything I was supposed to do and it's nearly home time so I didn't think it would matter.'

'Okay, who's there?'

'Ice cream.'

'Ice cream who?'

'Ice cream every time I see a ghost!'

The music that the principal, Bob Hamblin, had installed to signal a quiet end to the school day played gently in the corridor outside. The children knew the drill and began to pack up their pencils and put their drawings on Jacinta's desk.

'Okay, Nigel a good joke. Now put your drawing on my desk.'

'It was a very important joke, miss.' His little eyes were wide as he stood there, and Jacinta paused as his eyes filled with tears, 'Miss? Is my Mummy a ghost? Should I be scared at night?'

'No, sweetie, there's no such thing as ghosts.' She put her hands gently on both his shoulders, knowing now why it had taken him so long to ask her the knock-knock question.

His lips quivered as he smiled. 'Really?'

'No, Nigel, they are imaginary things in stories we read, and see in movies.' Jacinta was at a bit of a loss as to what to say to reassure him, but Nigel's little face brightened.

'Thank you, Miss. That's what I wanted to know. I won't be scared now.' Nigel took off for the door and as she stood and watched him go out to the corridor, he caught up with this older brother.

As Jacinta checked to see that all of the desks were clear, she made a note to catch Callie and tell her what Nigel had asked. She and Braden needed to be aware of what was going through his little head.

Once the room was packed up, she reached for her bag, deciding to go home early.

'Miss Mason?' Lisa, the administrative assistant always called the staff by their surnames during school hours.

'Hi, Lisa.'

Lisa looked around and checked the children had all gone. 'Jacinta, a guy called in and left a message for you at the front counter a while ago.'

'A guy?' Jacinta frowned. *Surely not.*

'Yes, he asked for your phone number but I didn't give it to him, so he left a message for you and said to give him a call. This is his number.'

She reached out and took the post-it note that Lisa held out. There would only be one person asking for her number. 'Thanks, Lisa. I'll give him a call when I get home.'

Lisa's eyes were full of curiosity and she waited a while, obviously hoping that Jacinta would explain or say who it was. 'He was a looker,' she said with a grin.

'Yes, Ryder is a fine-looking man.' A funny feeling ran through her. Saying his name made it feel real. 'Okay, see you tomorrow.'

'Bye. Have a good night.' Lisa winked at her.

'He's just an old friend from Brisbane. No need to look like that.' Jacinta forced a smile onto her face.

'Still a good looker, though.' Lisa grinned and disappeared up the corridor.

Jacinta's thoughts were jumbled as she walked home. She didn't bring her car to school unless she had to stay late for meetings; the short walk was a bit of exercise in her day.

Would she ring him back or not? What did he want? If he wanted to say something to her, why hadn't he come after her on Saturday night?

To be fair, Ryder had probably been as shocked to see her as she had been to see him come out into the beer garden where she'd been sitting.

Plus, she hadn't given him much of a chance to

come back and say anything. She'd taken off like a shot when he walked away. She could barely remember walking home.

All she could think of was Ryder was in town.

Jacinta bit her lip, knowing full well she would probably have to ring him.

Seeing Ryder in her town, and having him come looking for her, was a chance for closure. She needed it badly; she was never going to move on until she found out why he'd left her.

Maybe it would be hard. Maybe it was something she didn't want to know. Maybe there was something about her he didn't like. Maybe she hadn't been good enough in bed; that had always been uppermost in her mind, but she needed to hear it from him.

In a way, it would be good to hear what it had been, but even if he wouldn't tell her—and she knew the lovely guy she had fallen in love with wouldn't hurt her deliberately—she still wanted to know why on earth Ryder was working in a glorified strip show in the outback.

Jacinta shook her head she couldn't believe it. What on earth would his mother say, and who was taking Beryl for her Sunday outings? She and Ryder had taken his mother for a walk to South Bank every Sunday for the six months before the night he'd left her. Beryl had grown quieter over those months, but Jacinta had been too involved in talking to Ryder, to think about it. She'd just put it down to Beryl being comfortable in her company, and being happy that Ryder had listened to his mother's advice and had hooked up with Jacinta.

With a frown, she wondered if Beryl had passed and Ryder had had some sort of breakdown. Maybe he'd needed to get away?

There was no magic solution out west though. Even in a small region like Morweh Shire, people had breakdowns, marriages split, and children were left in single families. Jacinta still recalled the suicides during the drought a few years back.

Life was as tough, even tougher out here than it was in the city.

Even the strongest man could suffer and she

knew Ryder was strong and intelligent, but if he had trauma in his life, this might be his way of dealing with it.

The rain had cleared through the day but there was still a chill wind blowing and she wondered if he was in town. Or if they'd moved on. She hadn't been able to help herself. She'd Googled the dance show to see where it was going next and when.

Not that she had any intention of going to a show, even if she was curious. The next show was in Tambo tomorrow night, so there was a chance they were still in town. Then Blackall, and then Charleville.

If they had stayed in town, they were most likely staying at the pub, so she avoided that on the way from school to her apartment.

At home, she made a strong cup of coffee and composed herself before she took out his number.

Rather than just having a knee-jerk reaction to whatever he said, she'd have her answers ready and would think carefully about what she was going to tell him.

Not that it took much thinking.

I moved back to Augathella.

I rented an apartment.

I got a job at the school. I've been here ever since.

I have a boring life but I'm happy.

And no, I don't have a partner.

What else could he ask her?

And what was she going to ask him?

She didn't have to be truthful about what she needed. He didn't need to know that she wanted him still.

After almost three years.

All she wanted was to have one question answered.

Why did you leave me?

Hmm, probably a bit direct straight up

Maybe, what are you doing with your life these days, Ryder?

Well, that was obvious; he was working in the strip show.

Did you always have a hidden desire to be a

stripper, Ryder?

And that's what made no sense. He'd left the city. He'd left his mother, and he'd left a job that, as far as she knew, he really loved; a worthwhile and important job; doing cancer research at a prestigious institute. She'd Googled the institute yesterday to see if he was still on the staff, but his name or photo didn't appear on the staff page.

She had to think of more specific questions that he could answer with a proper explanation and not a simple yes or no. He was in town—her town—and she would get the truth.

Jacinta put her coffee cup in the sink and, as she reached for her phone, she thought of that morning she'd woken up alone.

Chapter 11

Her first call was to Sophie and Kent's place. Jacinta waited for her brother to pick up the call.

'Hey, Jace. How are you going? I haven't talked to you for a couple of weeks.'

'Hi, Kent, all good here. I've been pretty busy at school. I caught up with Soph at the pub the other night. I want to apologise to her for leaving early. I had something I had to do. I'll tell you about it later. Are you and Sophie home? I heard that you and the boys were mustering this week.'

'We are, but I'm home now. Sophie and I are about to leave for Charleville. We're meeting Ben and Amelia down there for dinner at the Corones Hotel.'

'Nice. Say hello from me. I have a favour to ask. Do you mind if I come home tonight seeing you're not there?'

'Sis, you don't have to ask that. It's your home too.'

'No, it's yours and Sophie's now. I just need somewhere private to talk to somebody. I don't want to stay in town.'

Kent laughed and Jacinta could almost see him waggling his eyebrows. 'That sounds a bit suss. How private? "Romantic assignation private?" What haven't you been telling us? Who's the lucky guy?'

'Nothing like that, big brother. Don't be silly. I'll tell you all about it afterwards. Give Sophie my love. Tell her I'm sorry I left her hen's night, but you'll understand why I did when I talk to you.'

'You're all right? You're not sick or anything?'

'No, I'm fine. Don't worry about me. I'll see you soon, okay?'

'Okay. You have me intrigued. Drive safe.'

'I will.'

'Love you, sis.'

'Love you too.'

No. I'm not sick, just a bit heartsick and nervous.

Jacinta glanced at the clock; it was only just

after four. If Ryder agreed to meet her there, she could be out at Lara Waters by a quarter to five, give him a cup of coffee, and then have a chat and send him on his way.

Then she'd be all sorted and life could get back to normal. Feeling more confident now that she had a plan in place, she picked up the phone and looked at the number on the post-it note.

Her heart and confidence plummeted again.

It was a different number from what it had been when they were together. No wonder she hadn't been able to contact him when she'd tried again a few weeks after he'd disappeared.

Don't be stupid. You were just a temporary girlfriend and you're making too much of it.

Her thoughts went back to that awful time. She'd overreacted; she should still be in Brisbane, working in a school and saving for her little house on the coast. It was all Ryder's fault; his actions had caused it all. She let her anger build and replace her wavering confidence.

Pressing the number into her phone, she held it

to her ear and waited before putting it down on the bench and turning the speaker on. Her hands were shaking too much to hold it.

Bloody wake up to yourself, girl. It's just a phone call.

The call rang for a long time and just before she was about to give up, the call picked up.

'Ryder Francesco speaking.'

Did she sense a little bit of hesitancy in his voice?

Perhaps.

'Ryder, it's Jacinta Mason here,' she said formally. Her voice was firm but distant.

'Oh, hello. Thanks for returning my call.'

She waited. She wasn't going to drive this conversation.

Not yet, anyway.

Finally, he broke the silence. 'I was hoping that we could meet in town this afternoon and have a bit of a chat. I need to talk to you, Jacinta.'

'Yes. And I need to talk to you, Ryder.' Her voice was still firm and she was in control.

'It would be good to have a bit of a catchup, don't you think?' he said.

There was another long silence and this time, Jacinta broke it. 'Not really a catch-up considering the circumstances, but I would like to speak to you,' she said.

'Yes.'

'I'm actually free now and I was wondering whether you'd meet me out at our family property.'

'I think…' he said slowly. 'I think I should be right to do that. I'll just have to check with somebody first.'

Somebody? Did he have a partner there with him? She hadn't thought of that.

Not that she'd seen anyone apart from Ryder and the guys on stage. Maybe they were part of a bigger group. There *had* been some unfamiliar faces in the crowd at the pub on Saturday night.

She'd kept such a low profile over the weekend she hadn't seen anyone.

'Well, if you can, we're about twenty kilometres out on the Southwest Road. The old Charleville

Road. When you get to the fork, you'll see a sign saying Kilcoy Station, and then you take the left turn there. Our place is about four or five kms along that road. You'll see a milk can letterbox with Lara Waters written on it. As far as I know, there aren't any locked gates at the moment, but—'

Ryder interrupted. 'I didn't think you lived out there. I mean I was talking to an old fellow in town the other night and he told me that you lived in town in an apartment.'

'Reg's been sharing the town details around as usual, has he? Well, Ryder, I've got no secrets. There's nothing new about me.'

Knowing that he'd been talking to Reg about her made her angry. What did he say? "Oh, an old girlfriend lives in town."

'So are you coming or not? I have other things I could be doing.'

'You can't meet me in town?'

Stuff it. She was calling the shots here.

'No, I'd prefer you to come out to the farm, please. Kent lives there now. Mum and Dad live in

Brisbane.' She paused, knowing it was nerves making her gabble on.

'Okay,' Ryder said. 'I'll be there. Just give me about an hour. If that's all right?'

'Yes, that's fine with me. You'll be right to get there?'

'Is the road okay?' he asked. 'We've been on some rough ones.'

'It's graded. I'll see you soon.'

'I'm looking forward to it, Jacinta.'

As Jacinta pressed disconnect on the phone, her hands were shaking. She pulled herself to task; she'd have time for a quick shower and then head straight out to Kent and Sophie's.

Her heart thudded as she walked into her bedroom and wondered what to wear.

Chapter 12

'Clive, I need a favour, mate.' Ryder spoke softly at the end of the bed in the emergency ward.

Clive was still in the ward with Bram because Dr Higgins said it was easier to have Bram in the cubicle at the far end of Emergency as he dealt with the other issues of the day. Bram had been there since they'd arrived last night and hadn't been admitted.

Clive had been in and out all day to give Ryder a break. Bram was in a normal sleep now and Ryder's heart clenched as he looked down at his younger brother.

His cheeks were pink compared to that awful yellow colour when he'd burst into Bram's room with Clive last night; his breathing was deep and even. His dark lashes blended with the shadows beneath his eyes.

He had the face of a model, and no one would ever know the demons that took hold of him and had led him into a life of substance abuse.

'He's going okay. The doc just said he could probably leave in a couple of hours.'

'A couple of hours? I have somewhere I have to be for about that long. Can you stay with him, Clive? Keep an eye on him. I'll get back by six-thirty at the latest. I'm sorry, but I have to go out. I'll be taking the van if any of the boys are looking for it.'

'They won't be. When I went back, they were playing pool and settled in for the night. Do what you have to, Ryder. I'm sweet to stay here.'

'I know the medical staff are here but I'd hate him to wake up and think he was by himself again,' Ryder said.

'Or do another runner,' Clive said, shaking his head.

'We owe you big time, Clive.'

'Maybe. But you and I—and Bram, a bit later—are going to sit down and have a chat in the next few days.'

Ryder ran his hand through his hair. 'I know. I

need to do something.'

Bram's addiction had started in his mid-teens, not long after their father had been killed in a car accident.

Ryder hadn't ever been given much information back then—it was as though Mum thought if she didn't talk about it, the problem would go away. All he knew was that Mum had found a summons pushed down behind Bram's chest of drawers. A summons for a court appearance he hadn't told anyone about and had skipped. The next thing Ryder knew was the police knocking on the door, and Mum sent him to the backyard. When he came back inside, Bram had gone.

He didn't come home for a month; in later years Ryder discovered that he'd been admitted to a juvenile mental health facility in an attempt to treat him.

'I'll be as quick as I can,' he said to Clive now. 'I'm grateful, mate.'

'Don't worry, we won't leave until you get back.'

With a sigh, Ryder turned away. He would look after Bram; he always had, even before he'd promised Mum.

##

Ryder had a quick shower and shave; he felt as though he'd been living in the same clothes for days.

Everything was crushed in his suitcase so he went looking in the antique wardrobe and found an iron and a small ironing board, and quickly pressed a clean pair of jeans and a black T-shirt. Once he was dressed, he went back into the bathroom and flicked a comb over hair that was in need of a trim. Then he splashed some aftershave on. Probably smelled off, the bottle was over two years old.

But it was too late now.

He picked up his boots and nerves took hold as he sat on the side of the bed and pulled his socks on. He had to think about what he was going to say, and he also had to be prepared for any questions Jacinta might ask. He'd say that he changed careers and had to travel. But that didn't explain why he hadn't contacted her until he'd stumbled upon her little town.

Why couldn't he just tell Jacinta the truth?

He paused in the middle of putting the second sock on and thought about it. Truth be known, he was ashamed of what he'd done. There was no excuse for the way he'd treated her; he'd simply taken the cowardly way out.

He wasn't ashamed of promising Mum that he'd look after Bram. He'd decided to get Bram away from the city, but that meant Ryder had to leave his job.

He was embarrassed to let Jacinta know that he'd stuffed up so badly. Three wasted years, because his strategy had failed and that had made him realise what poor decisions he'd made.

Until today, Bram had been good for three months. He must've found what he was always looking for out at the shearing shed. But what were the chances of that?

Knowing Bram, he'd probably made a call to

find out contacts and organise them to meet him out there.

Who knew? There was nothing more that could be done about it now.

Move on, keep him clean. As he'd tried to for the past two and a half years. For a while, he'd kidded himself it had been working, but he knew now that Bram had deceived him on several occasions. Hindsight was a fine thing.

The main thing he had to focus on now, was the present.

And the future. Looking back gained nothing. The most important thing was to make amends to Jacinta this evening.

Then move on again. For how many years? What sort of future was he looking at? Would Mum really have wanted him to do this? To waste his life? Because he knew now that what he was doing was achieving nothing. He was simply marking time until the next overdose.

Ryder closed his eyes.

How much closer can I watch him?

Almost bloody impossible.

Half an hour later as Ryder had left the hospital, Bram stirred and called him back.

'I'm really sorry, Ryder. I didn't mean to do it. I'm a useless bastard. I'm sorry. I won't do it again.'

It was probably the tenth time Ryder had heard that over the past few years.

Chapter 13

By the time Jacinta arrived at Lara Waters, Kent and Sophie had left for Charleville. She was pleased she'd arranged to meet Ryder here. It was her territory and a place she felt safe.

Calm stole over her as soon as she drove through the front gate.

Growing up on the station had been wonderful and it had made her the woman she was now. The station held wonderful memories and she let those happy memories from the days before she went to Brisbane and met Ryder fill her thoughts now.

As she thought about it, she realised she hadn't regained any feeling of happiness since he'd left her. She had just let herself exist and go through the motions.

It was time to deal with that.

The realisation filled her with new strength and she knew—hoped—as soon as they had this conversation, she would be able to get over him.

But she was going to demand some answers. If he just hadn't wanted to have a permanent relationship, she wanted to know if she had done something wrong.

She knew she could take it and then get over him. She'd played this dreaming game for too long. Deep down, she'd always hoped that he would come back and say sorry, and they'd get back together.

And that made her angry. She was weak.

Parking the car near the shed, Jacinta opened the gate to the house yard; she smiled at the pretty display of flowers.

Sophie had been working hard, and Jacinta felt guilty that she hadn't come out here more often. Kent and Sophie tended to come into town to the pub to catch up with her and have a meal together. Sometimes Sophie would wait for her after school and they would go for a coffee.

It looked like she'd been very busy out here. Mum would be pleased; the garden was beautiful.

And that was another worry that was always

niggling at the back of her mind, and Jacinta hadn't given it enough attention either. When she banished Ryder Francesco from her life once and for all, she would focus on her family. She'd go to Brisbane next school holidays and spend the time with her parents. Kent had said they'd moved there because it was closer to medical care. Jacinta knew every time she asked Mum how Dad was, the reassurance was maybe for her benefit. When Mum said Dad was fine, she didn't quite believe her. Nevertheless, they'd be home for the wedding in a couple of weeks and she could suss Dad out then.

Anyway, if she went to Brisbane in the holidays, she wouldn't have to worry about bumping into Ryder now; it seemed there was more chance of that happening out here.

Him and that stupid strip show.

Jacinta found the spare key under the mat where it always was and unlocked the front door. As she went inside and looked around, she could see that Sophie had already put her own personal touches on the house, which was good because she knew

Sophie had doubts.

'It's your Mum and Dad's house,' she'd said over coffee one day.

'No, you and Kent are managing the property now and it's your home. Mum would be really pleased to see that you're changing it around to suit you and Kent.' Jacinta chuckled. Mum wasn't the best interior designer anyway, but she'd loved her garden.

Colourful throw rugs sat on the back of the old sofas, and there were a couple of new prints on the wall. All the while Jacinta was taking this in, it stopped her from thinking about the talk ahead.

Sophie must have picked some flowers knowing that she was coming to visit because even though they were going to be away for a few days, there was a bunch of freshly picked roses on the kitchen bench.

Okay, the kitchen would be good; they could sit on either side of the table and she could offer Ryder a coffee.

Opening the pantry, she checked the biscuit

barrel was full, put the kettle on, and pulled out two mugs and some sugar.

She smoothed her hands down the front of her dress and was pleased to see that they weren't shaking.

Yet.

Coming home and seeing Ryder here on her territory had been the right choice.

***

Ryder followed Jacinta's directions and it only seemed a short time before he turned onto the road that led to Lara Waters.

He had composed himself on the drive out, thinking of all the times he'd spent with her and how he hadn't seen her for two and a half years. Even though he felt sad and he thought about her all the time, he'd learned to live with it.

He might not be coping and this existence might not be what he wanted his life to be, but that was the way things had panned out.

He owed Jacinta an apology for the way he'd left her. He could tell by the way she had spoken to him on Saturday night that he wasn't her favourite person. Getting closer, he gripped the steering wheel.

Then again, maybe his ego was getting in the way. Maybe she'd moved on straightaway; at least he knew she wasn't married, according to old Reg.

And he was pretty sure that Reg knew what was going on in town.

Maybe she hadn't given him much thought after the first week or two. Hopefully talking out their breakup would give them both closure—if she needed it—and if he apologised, he'd feel better.

They could have a brief talk, even though he wondered why he had to have it out here when she was living in town.

Maybe her brother was here and she was using him as protection not knowing what Ryder was like these days.

The thought of Jacinta not trusting him hurt, and he briefly closed his eyes and then opened them, realising he should be watching the road closely.

He huffed out a sigh. He knew exactly what he wanted. He wanted Jacinta, he wanted his old life back, he wanted to be working at the Institute and he wanted Mum to be alive.

But the chances of any of those things happening were as likely as Mum coming back from the dead.

Ryder realised that Bram hadn't come into his thoughts; it was because his brother's addiction and the care of Bram had consumed him for the last two and a half years.

He didn't want to be doing it but he'd promised and he had to keep that promise.

A pair of gates was just ahead on the left and he spotted the Lara Waters sign just in time to slow down and turn into the property. A winding driveway crested a hill; something rare out in this flat outback landscape.

As he approached the house built on another small rise, Ryder noticed a small red Hyundai parked outside and he assumed that that was

Jacinta's car.

His mouth dried and he swallowed; it would be just his luck if his throat closed up and he couldn't tell her what he needed to say.

And he still hadn't figured out how he was going to say what he had to say. He'd just go from the heart and wing it.

No, he wouldn't go from the heart; if he went from his heart, he'd be putting his arms around her and holding her close.

And that certainly *wasn't* going to happen.

***

When Jacinta heard a vehicle coming up the drive she walked to the front window and stood behind the curtain.

A white van was halfway up the driveway and as she watched, it pulled up next to her Hyundai.

As she expected, when the door opened, Ryder stepped out. He stood next to the car and looked over at the house for a moment before putting his hands in his jeans pockets and walking casually over to the gate.

Her heart beat faster as she watched him. Tall and broad-shouldered as he always had been, he looked as if he'd lost some weight since she'd last seen him. She hadn't noticed in the dark the other night that his face was a little gaunt.

She hoped he hadn't been ill.

But then again if he was working for a dance troupe and getting a lot of exercise and practice; it made sense that he lost weight keeping fit.

She shook her head, still not being able to understand why he had chosen a job like that.

As he approached the house, Jacinta hurried down the hall to the front door, her hands shaking.

Deep breaths, she told herself.

It would be best to wait out on the veranda for him but he was too quick. Just as she opened the door, she heard his footsteps coming up the front stairs.

By the time she had the door open, he was already at the top and she stepped outside. They stood there for a moment and looked at each other. As she held his eyes, a huge shaft of heat struck her in the chest.

Panic filled her.

I should have just ignored his message. She should have just let him leave her town, and go back out into his life.

The only thing she wanted now was to have his arms around her, and she would rest against his chest.

She tried to look away but Ryder's expression made her head spin. He was looking at her like he used to.

They both stepped towards each other at the same time and as his hand took hers, a shock went right up her arm.

'Hello, Jacinta.' His voice was as deep and husky as always. 'It's really good to see you again.'

'It's good to have you here.' Her voice was trembling and she knew she was on the verge of tears.

Why did she say that? Because it wasn't good,

all she wanted to do was be in Ryder's arms. It was as though the past two years disappeared, and he hadn't left her. Jacinta's need was deep and visceral, and she knew when he left her again, she wouldn't cope.

'Are you all right?' he said.

Her eyes filled with tears and she shook her head mutely.

Ever so slowly, Ryder took a step forward and then she was in his arms, her head on his chest as the familiar smell of his citrus cologne surrounded her.

He lowered his head and rested his forehead against hers just like they'd stood together, and danced together, in the past. Her arms wrapped around his neck. She closed her eyes and inhaled the comforting fragrance.

She wouldn't let herself think. She simply lived in the moment. Her heart was telling her she shouldn't be doing this, but when his forehead touched hers, she was lost.

Jacinta clung to him and he held her tightly and

neither of them said a word. They stood together for a few minutes.

Ryder's breathing was deep and even, but eventually, he moved and turned away from her. Her heart broke all over again.

'I'm so sorry, Jacinta. I had no right to do that. Please forgive me. I had no intention—'

She looked away and said quietly. 'I forgive you, Ryder. For all of it.'

Lifting her eyes again, she looked at him and could see the deep shadows beneath his eyes. This wasn't the Ryder she had known. Ryder with a smooth face and happy smile; he'd aged and there were new wrinkles around his eyes.

He spoke again and took another step away from her. 'I couldn't help myself.'

'I told you it was all right.' Her voice was tentative. 'I know exactly how you felt. Or I hope that you know how I feel, and that you were feeling the same?'

Lifting her chin a little bit higher, she tried to think, but all the questions she'd thought of had gone.

All Jacinta wanted to know. . . all she needed to know, was simple.

'Ryder. I'm only going to ask you one thing. Will you be honest with me?' Her voice shook and she cleared her throat. 'Please.'

'I'll try to be as honest with you as I can,' he said.

'I want you . . .' she stumbled over the words, 'I want you to tell me what you're feeling at this exact moment because I'm sensing the very last thing I expected.'

He stared at her and ran both hands over his hair.

'You want me to be honest?'

'Yes, I do.'

'All right. This is what I've dreamed about for the past two years six months and one week, Jacinta.'

'So why?' she whispered. 'Why did you leave me?'

'I can't... I couldn't... I mean...I haven't—'

She kept her eyes on his face.

'Shit,' he said. 'This is exactly why I didn't come back to you. We can't do this. I always knew that if I came back to you I wouldn't be able to—'

'Wouldn't be able to what? You're totally confusing me, Ryder.'

His voice was almost a whisper. 'I've never stopped loving you, Jacinta.'

Her heart jumped at his words and she took a step towards him but he held up his hand.

'I know I hurt you, and there's no point in telling you now. I've really stuffed this up. I only came here to apologise, to give us closure finally, but being with you, seeing you, holding you … I didn't think this through. But it doesn't mean things are going to be any different.'

'I don't understand. You never told me you loved me when we were together and now you're saying that you do, but we can't be together. What do you mean?'

'It's not just us, Jacinta. I have to consider others.'

She pushed her hands against his chest and he held them against him. 'No, that's total bullshit.' Her voice was shrill. 'A copout. Why don't you just say that you came here to see how I was and to make yourself feel better?'

'Well, you're spot on there,' he said. 'Except for the last bit. I told you, I've never stopped loving you.'

Tears spilled over and ran down her cheeks. 'If that's true, what's the problem? Because, Ryder, I have never forgotten you in the two years and however many months and days it's been. You've been in my heart every second of every day. And I can't stand to lose you all over again. My life has been on hold and when I saw you in the pub the other night, I couldn't believe it. I was going to ignore it and hope you went away and I didn't see you, but when I got your message at the school, I knew I had to talk to you. For my sanity and closure and now what have you done? You come in here and you tell me that you love me but we can't be together. What the hell am I supposed to think?'

With a ragged groan, Ryder let go of her hands and took her in his arms again.

'If I tell you, you're going to want me to make some changes and I can't do that.'

'You're talking rubbish. I don't understand. Can you please tell me what's wrong with you? Are you sick? Why are you working as a stripper?'

His eyes widened and he went to speak, but she talked over him.

'You've got no idea what has happened to my confidence since you left. I thought it was because I didn't measure up to your standards when we slept together that last night before you left. I woke up the next morning and I thought you'd be back. I thought you were going to get me a coffee or breakfast. I lay there and I waited for you for two hours. And then I got out of bed and had a shower and I tried to call you.' Tears welled over again. 'And your phone had a different message. The message that told me . . . *me* . . . that you were not available for a few *months*. It was as though it was recorded just for me.'

She looked up at him. 'And so I knew exactly where I stood.'

Chapter 14

Ryder held Jacinta close as her voice quavered and tears rolled down her cheeks.

'I love you, Jacinta. Just hold onto that first. I'll tell you everything you need to know.'

She smiled through her tears.

'Leaving you that morning was one of the hardest and most foolish things I've ever done. I thought I could walk away and we'd both get over it. I knew I had to give you up. I knew you'd want to come with me, and I wasn't going to allow that.'

Her heart beat hard, as she struggled to understand what he was saying.

'Go where? Wait,' she said. 'I think we need to sit down and I'll make us a coffee, and you can tell me exactly what you're talking about. And then if you have to leave me after that, at least I'll understand.'

'I will have to leave you. You need to know that. I won't subject you to the life I lead these days.'

She took his hand and led Ryder into the kitchen. 'Sit there while I make us coffee and hold that last thing you said. You *are* going to tell me why. And just for the record, if I had to, I could cope with you being a stripper.'

Finally, a smile creased his cheeks, and it was *her* Ryder looking at her. 'First thing. I'm not a stripper.'

'A male dancer, then.' The kettle came back to a boil and Jacinta poured hot water onto the instant coffee, added one sugar and milk to both of them and put the mug in front of him.

Sitting down, she wrapped her hand around her mug. If she held that and stayed on this side of the table, she wouldn't want to touch him. A tendril of hope unfurled in her chest, and she was determined that, whatever he said, she would make him see reason.

'Hang on.' An unbidden thought came into her head. 'Are you married? Is there someone else? Did someone have your child before we met?'

He went to reach over to her, but she kept her

hands around the warm mug. Leaning back again, Ryder reached for his coffee.

'First thing. I'm *not* a stripper or a dancer. I work on the road crew for the show.'

'But my friend said your name was on the program. You were the cowboy.'

'Did you see me on stage?'

'Yes, and I left. I wasn't sure if it was you but I didn't want to risk it.'

Then you saw my brother, Bram, on stage.'

'Your brother? What brother?'

'My younger brother. He looks very much like me. Jace? Let me start at the beginning. Then you'll understand why I can't have you in my life. When it all started, and I had to go to the hospital—'

'You *are* sick!'

'Please listen. I'm trying to put this into context when all I bloody want to do is come over there and lift you onto my lap and kiss you senseless.'

Jacinta sat quietly sipping her coffee, as Ryder told her about Beryl dying, and how he'd sat with her. How his mother had extracted a promise from him on her deathbed to look after Bram and keep him on the straight and narrow.

'I couldn't do that in the city. I couldn't go to work every day and leave him. I knew we'd have to leave and we moved to a station out west for a while. There was nowhere he could get drugs out there. After a couple of months, his former employer rang and asked me if he was straight again. Bram has been an addict since he was sixteen, and it wasn't a secret. He's been given so many chances and screwed up every one. So, I guess you can say I'm his minder. Shit!'

Jacinta jumped as Ryder looked at his watch. 'I have to go to the hospital.'

'Why?' She frowned.

'Because he overdosed last night, and Dr Higgins is going to discharge him tonight. I have to be there with him.'

'Ryder? There has to be another way. You can't be his minder for the rest of his life.'

His smile was bitter. 'And that's exactly what I knew you'd say. I promised my mother, Jacinta. I can't break that promise.'

Her voice was soft. 'You honoured that promise at the expense of your life, your career,' her voice broke, 'and our love. You've given it your best shot. Isn't it time to think of yourself, Ryder?'

He shook his head. 'I have to go.'

Pushing the chair out, he stood and looked at her for a moment before he came around to her and took the mug from her hands.

She froze, her limbs stiff in his hold, but her body swayed towards him as though a magnetic force was pulling her close.

One hand moved to cup her cheek, and her heart broke as she saw tears in Ryder's eyes.

'This is goodbye, Jacinta.' Her lips opened in anticipation as he lowered his head to hers, and her mouth was gently touched by his warm, loving lips.

Chapter 15

Two days later

'Jacinta Mason, you are full of surprises.' Bec Hunter looked at her from the passenger seat of the Hyundai as they sped up the highway. 'Why won't you tell me why we're going to the male revue at the Tambo Hotel?'

Jacinta smiled sweetly, and Bec shook her head.

'Last week you were a cot case and wouldn't go within cooee of that show. What's happened?'

'I'm going to convince the man who loves me that he can't live without me.' Jacinta grinned at the look on Bec's face.

'Right, that makes sense. Not.'

Half an hour later, they parked near the Tambo Library. Cars lined both sides of the highway as they walked to the hotel famous for its nightly chicken races. A huge brown dog with drooping jaws stood in the doorway and flicked them a disinterested glance.

The front bar of the pub was empty. 'Are you

sure it's here and not at the club?' Bec said.

The guy behind the bar looked over and Jacinta saw Bec do a double take. 'You're in the right place, ladies. Show me your tickets and I'll let you out the back. The races are over and the show is about to start on the grass.'

'Tickets?' Bec said.

'On my phone.' Jacinta showed the screen to the guy who was staring at Bec. He looked away from her and looked briefly at the two tickets that Jacinta had downloaded.

'And who is who?' he asked with a roguish grin. 'Now let me guess, you're Jacinta, and you're Bec.'

'Very clever,' Bec replied drily, but she was smiling. 'And you are?'

'Matt. Matt Randall. Are you really sure you want to go and see that show? You could stay in here and talk to me.'

Bec flicked a glance at Jacinta. 'I did see it last week.'

'And it was so good, you wanted to come back?' Matt said.

'Um,' Bec said.

'She's here to provide moral support for me.' Jacinta rolled her eyes. 'Stay here if you want to. I'm going to see the show I missed last week. I'll be back later, Bec.' She shook her head and grinned as she walked through to the lawn out the back of the pub.

Double rows of seats surrounded a square patch of lawn where a makeshift stage had been set up. Her gaze honed straight in on Ryder who was standing beside an older guy.

'Okay, Ryder. The fun begins.' She made her way around the back of the stands. The sun had set and the night was cool as dark began to fall. She wasn't looking forward to the drive back to Augathella in the dark.

Ryder had made his promise, but so had she. Jacinta was not going to let him go again.

As she was almost to him, he looked up and their eyes locked. At first, he smiled instinctively and then a frown creased his brow.

'Hello, Ryder,' she said, standing on her toes

and brushing a brief kiss across his mouth.

'Jacinta! What are you doing here?' he asked.

'I came to see the show.' She put her hand on his arm. 'Oh, and to tell you something.'

'Tell me something?' he said slowly.

'Yes. I thought you should know I'm not giving up.'

'What do you mean?'

'If I have to follow you from Augathella to Atherton, or from Dirranbandi to Duckinwilla, I will. I'm not letting you go, Ryder.'

His mouth spread in a grin. 'You have such a way with words. You always did. And the answer's no. I haven't changed my mind.'

'You will. Where are we going next?'

'Where are *we* going?' His eyes were wide.

'Yes, I've taken some leave from work, and it's the school holidays next week. I don't have to be back for two weeks until Kent and Sophie's wedding.'

'You can't.'

'I can and I did. Now, where's my seat?

'Jacinta. You can't do this.'

'Do you love me?'

'You know I do.'

'Well, I can. I just have to take Bec home tonight, and then I'll meet up wherever you are tomorrow.'

'Who's Bec? And, Jacinta, you can't. You can't give up your job and your life.'

'Bec's my friend and she's in there chatting up the barman. And I can, you know.'

'What? Chat the barman up?' Ryder frowned.

'No. Give my life up. You did, didn't you, Ryder?'

'No.'

'We can do it together.'

A voice came from behind her. 'Well said, lass. Finally, someone might be able to talk sense into that thick head.'

'Where's Bram?' Ryder said. 'Jacinta, this is Clive, the manager.'

She held out her hand and Clive shook it. 'Bram's getting ready with the rest of the guys. Stop worrying.'

'Right, I'll go and do the sound check. Jacinta, we'll talk later.'

***

Saturday night

Jacinta hadn't waited to talk to Ryder after the Tambo show. She collected a reluctant Bec from the bar and headed home before the show finished. She had a plan.

'God, he was an interesting guy.'

'Who?' Jacinta, asked absently, her mind on Ryder and the encouraging words that Clive had said when he'd sat with her for a while in the break between sets.

'Matt. A real free spirit, just working his way around the world. Just him and a backpack.'

'Nice for some.'

'He's going to come to Augathella next. I told him there's always bar work there.'

'Bit smitten, love?'

'No, he was just an interesting guy.'

Jacinta rolled her eyes. 'Have you got plans for Saturday night?'

'Yeah, I'm working with the locum. Dr Harry and Laura are going to Longreach for a medical conference. Why, what's on?'

'I'm going to Charleville to the revue.'

'What, the same one you just saw? What did you think of it anyway?'

'It was good. It's more entertaining watching the audience though.'

'So why are you going to see it again? Have you sorted out whatever it was that upset you last week?'

'I have. Ryder just has to realise I'm not letting him go.'

'You go, girl.' Bec's grin was full of mischief. 'You should stay overnight at the Corones Hotel. The rooms there are fabulous.'

'Sounds like a plan.'

'I hope it all works out for you, Jace. You look so much happier now.'

'It will. I'm not giving up, Bec.'

Chapter 16

Charleville, Saturday night.

Ryder kept an eye on the women as they came into the club. Jacinta had thrown him for a spin last Tuesday, turning up at Tambo, and he wouldn't put it past her to arrive tonight.

He scanned the crowd and spotted her. She was waving at him, her smile wide, and his heart clenched.

God, he loved her and seeing her again had woken something inside him.

Bloody hell. The sooner they moved away from the west, the better. She would have to leave him alone. He didn't believe a word of what she said about following them from Dirranbandi to wherever.

His week had been good and bad. He'd missed Jacinta like crazy and then he'd been cross when she'd turned up. But he'd been even more out of sorts when he discovered she'd left Tambo without saying goodbye. He'd been looking forward to kissing her goodnight, so it was just as well she'd gone.

Yesterday, Larry had rung up from the Institute, begging him to come back. Clive had sat him down last night and tore strips off him, telling Ryder what a fool he'd been.

'But a fool with his heart in the right place,' Clive said.

Bram had been extra quiet all week, and Ryder had watched him carefully.

And now Jacinta had turned up. She'd soon get sick of him pushing her away.

'Ryder?'

He turned. Bram was standing beside him.

'Jeez, Bram. You better hurry and get dressed. The rest of the boys are ready to go on.'

'I'm not going on.'

'Why, are you all right?'

Clive came up behind Bram and put his hand on his shoulder. He was carrying a suitcase.

'What's going on?'

'You're in charge until I get back, Ryder,' Clive

said. 'And then you can call your boss in Brisbane and tell him you'll be back. Bram's leaving the troupe, and I'm sacking you.'

'What the hell?'

Bram spoke quietly. 'It's about time I took some real responsibility for my actions, Ryder. I've booked myself into a rehab clinic in Brisbane for three months. Clive and I are getting the seven o'clock flight to Brisbane. Taxi's waiting.'

Ryder didn't know what to say. He looked over and caught Jacinta watching them, and he could see straightaway that she knew.

'Does Jacinta have anything to do with this?' he asked.

'No, it was all my decision,' Bram said. 'But she knows. She's a good woman, Ryder. You'd be crazy to let her go.'

The lights dimmed and the opening guitar riff filled the club. Shrill cheers filled the break in the music.

'I don't know what to say,' Ryder said. 'I'll walk you out.'

Bram hugged him tightly and didn't speak again as he climbed into the taxi.

Clive shook his hand and reassured him. 'He'll be right. I won't leave until he's settled. Now it's over to you. Get that lady back, and ring up Larry.'

Ryder stood there until the tail lights of the taxi disappeared into the darkness. He turned to go back inside, but Jacinta was standing on the footpath waiting for him.

'Hello,' he said, his heart bursting with joy. She held her arms open and ran across to him and jumped into his arms. He lifted her and stared into her beautiful eyes. 'Jacinta Mason, my love. I just got the sack from my job. I have nothing to offer you but my love, but will you marry me? Will you be my wife ... and my life?'

'I'm so glad you finally accepted I wasn't going to go away,' she said as she lifted her face to his. 'I knew you couldn't push me away forever.'

'I'm never going to let you go,' he murmured against her lips. 'Will you move to Brisbane with me?'

'I was going to ask you to move to Brisbane with me,' she said with a laugh.

She stood on her toes and pressed her lips against his, and Ryder's life was complete.

Behind them came the raucous squeals of the Charleville crowd as Hilly, Chappo and Slim strutted their stuff.

'The show must go on,' he said, thinking of Bram and the brave decision he had made.

'Our life will go on,' Jacinta said. 'As long as we're together, we can face anything, my love.'

Epilogue

Spring arrived in Augathella to a flurry of warm breezes, clear blue skies, lush green paddocks, and a beautiful display of flowers in Jenny Riley's garden.

Jenny arrived at Lara Waters with boxes of freshly picked flowers, late on the morning of Kent and Sophie's wedding and was greeted by Kent's parents and Braden Cartwright.

'Hi, Jenny, where do you want us to put these? Do they need to be kept cool or watered?' Olivia Mason asked.

'No, Liv, all good. If the boys can carry the boxes to the breezeway, I'll start setting up.' Jenny reached into a small box. 'Here are the buttonhole posies for the groom and his mates, and here's your corsage.' She held out a small pale pink orchid.

'An orchid? Already? Jenny, you are a whizz with your garden.'

'It's been a good winter,' Jenny said. 'And my new conservatory protects my fragile plants from the worst of the winter and the heat of summer. The girls were really happy with the bouquet too.'

'How's Sophie?' Olivia asked quietly as Braden and Maso carried the first boxes from the back of the station wagon to the breezeway.

Jenny chuckled. 'The girls have taken over Jacinta's apartment and they look beautiful, and as happy as. The photographer had just arrived when I dropped off the bouquet. Your daughter is fair glowing. And Sophie has a dreamy smile on her face, but I do think she's a little bit nervous.'

'So's Kent. He and his groomsmen had a beer to take the edge off. Or that's what he said!' Olivia smiled. 'I haven't seen Jacinta so happy for a long time. Since Ryder came back on the scene, she's a different person. And did she tell you she's already got a job in Brisbane?'

'She did and I saw the beautiful engagement ring. Do you think they'll come back here for their wedding?'

'They will and they've already set the date. Jacinta wanted Sophie's wedding done with before she talked to you about flowers. It's an Easter wedding.'

'Fabulous. I'll make sure my autumn flowers are planted out early. Now come on, show me where the ceremony is and I'll get the flowers arranged.'

##

The mood was joyous as Kent and Ben, the best man, and the two groomsmen stood facing the guests before the ceremony began. Braden leaned down and whispered in Petie's ear. 'Now you have to be quiet when Callie walks down the aisle first. No calling out, okay?'

'Okay, Daddy.'

'And Nigel. You are to be on your very best behaviour.'

'Yes, Dad.'

Rory stood on his toes and whispered in Braden's ear. 'You don't have to tell me, Dad. I know.'

'Good man.' Braden looked down at his three little men. They each wore long trousers, white shirts and bow ties, and his heart was full of pride. He and Callie were doing well.

Braden's eyes pricked as Whitney Houston's memorable, *I Will Always Love You,* began to play.

Kent turned around and watched as first Callie, Jacinta and then Kimberley walked down the aisle between the rows of chairs in the garden.

Callie turned and smiled at Braden and the boys as she passed the aisle where they stood. A wave of love surged through him and he blew her a kiss.

A collective sigh sounded as Sophie walked down the aisle. Her eyes stayed on Kent's the whole way.

##

Three hours later the reception was in full swing. The meal had been served and exclaimed over, the speeches were over and the temporary dance floor was packed. The bride and groom were in each other's arms dancing to a slow romantic tune.

Old Reg had been invited to the wedding and

his eyes were alive with interest as he watched the proceedings from his chair in prime position close to the bridal table.

Romance was in the air.

He'd been right with the girl of Mason, and that dancer fella. They were engaged now.

He grinned and nodded as he watched Doc Higgins guide the New Zealand woman behind a potted palm and swoop her into a long kiss. Nurse Adnum was flushed when they reappeared. She waved to Reg when she saw him watching. Reg liked her; Laura always stopped to talk to him.

Reg smiled when he saw Ben Riley kneel down in front of that pretty Amelia who'd spent time chatting to Reg at the billy cart races last Easter. Looked like there was another wedding going to happen in Augathella.

The other nurse from the hospital caught Reg's attention as she ran into the marquee. She grabbed the doctor's arm and spoke urgently to him. No one else noticed Harry Higgins hurry outside.

Reg's curiosity got the better of him, and he

stood and shuffled outside. He needed to know everything that happened at the wedding so he could tell his stories at the pub next week.

A small group was gathered over at the back of the shed where the kids had been playing. Braden Cartwright was holding his youngest boy.

That drifter fellow who'd been playing the guitar in the pub for the last week or so lay on the ground. The doc and Nurse Hunter knelt beside him.

Reg's eyes widened as he saw the spreading pool of blood under the fella's head.

The last thing Augathella needed was a death at a wedding, Reg thought as he headed inside.

.

UNTIL THE NEXT STORY…

Callie, Fallon, Sophie, Amelia, Laura and Jacinta's stories continue in *Outback Dust* as we learn more about those who live in the district and those who come for a visit. Will the charms of

Augathella keep them there?

Coming in January 2023

Bec Hunter, an Augathella local and nurse at the local health centre, is driven by a strong work ethic and commitment to her career. Working and studying for a Master's degree in aged care leaves her little time for socialising. She has a life plan that does not include a relationship.

Travelling guitarist, Matt Randall, is new to town and doesn't intend to stay long, but his plans are thrown into turmoil when he is injured rescuing Petie Cartwright and is admitted to the health centre.

Intense chemistry sparks between patient and nurse. Bec pretends indifference to the newcomer, and Matt fights his attraction to the feisty nurse.

Will they overcome their differences as fate throws them together at every turn?

Outback Dust is available in:

eBook: https://books2read.com/u/bP7D9A

Print: https://www.annieseaton.net/store.html

The Augathella Girls series.

Book 1: Outback Roads –The Nanny
Book 2: Outback Sky – The Pilot
Book 3: Outback Escape – The Sister
Book 4: Outback Winds – The Jillaroo
Book 5: Outback Dawn – The Visitor
Book 6: Outback Moonlight – The Rogue
Book 7: Outback Dust – The Drifter
Book 8: Outback Hope – The Farmer

OTHER BOOKS from ANNIE

Whitsunday Dawn

Undara

Osprey Reef

East of Alice (November 2022)

Porter Sisters Series

Kakadu Sunset

Daintree

Diamond Sky

Hidden Valley

Larapinta

Pentecost Island Series

Pippa

Eliza

Nell

Tamsin

Evie

Cherry

Odessa

Sienna

Tess

Isla

Also available in three boxed sets

Books 1-3

Books 4-6

Books 7-10

The Augathella Girls Series

Outback Roads

Outback Sky

Outback Escape

Outback Wind

Outback Dawn

Outback Moonlight

Outback Dust

Outback Hope

Sunshine Coast Series

Waiting for Ana

The Trouble with Jack

Healing His Heart

Sunshine Coast Boxed Set

The Richards Brothers Series

The Trouble with Paradise

Marry in Haste

Outback Sunrise

Richards Brothers Boxed Set

Bondi Beach Love Series

Beach House

Beach Music

Beach Walk

Beach Dreams

The House on the Hill

Second Chance Bay Series

Her Outback Playboy

Her Outback Protector

Her Outback Haven

Her Outback Paradise

The McDougalls of Second Chance Bay Boxed Set

Love Across Time Series

Come Back to Me

Follow Me

Finding Home

The Threads that Bind

Love Across Time 1-4 Boxed Set

Bindarra Creek

Worth the Wait

Full Circle

Secrets of River Cottage (Nov 22)

Four Seasons Short and Sweet

Ten Days in Paradise

Follow the Sun

Others

Deadly Secrets

Adventures in Time

Silver Valley Witch

The Emerald Necklace

Christmas with the Boss

Her Christmas Star

An Aussie Christmas Duo (the two Christmas novellas)

A Clever Christmas

About the Author

Annie lives in Australia, on the beautiful north coast of New South Wales. She sits in her writing chair and looks out over the tranquil Pacific Ocean.

She writes contemporary romance and loves telling stories that always have a happily ever after. She lives with her very own hero of many years and they share their home with Toby, the naughtiest dog in the universe, and Barney, the ragdoll puss, who hides when the four grandchildren come to visit.

Stay up to date with her latest releases at her website: http://www.annieseaton.net

Milton Keynes UK
Ingram Content Group UK Ltd.
UKHW031312270824
1399UKWH00055B/416

9 780645 484311